Buy Another Day

MRD Enterprises, Inc.
PO BOX 1000
Mount Jackson, VA 22844
mrdenter@shentel.net

Library of Congress Registration Number: TXu2-099-436
ISBN978-0-692-13096-4

Contact author at info@michaelrdavidson.com

Cover by Rena Hoberman
http://www.coverquill.com

Printed and bound in the United States of America.

First printing 2018

Books by Michael R. Davidson

Harry's Rules

Incubus

The Incubus Vendetta

Caliphate – The Inquisitor and the Maiden

Caliphate - Retribution

Krystal

Eye for an Eye

The Dove

The Dead Lawyer

By Michael R. Davidson
&
Kseniya Kirillova

In the Shadow of Mordor

Successor

BUY ANOTHER DAY

By

Michael R. Davidson

MRD Enterprises, Inc.

2018

CAST OF MAIN CHARACTERS AND ORGANIZATIONS IN ORDER OF APPEARANCE

Vinogradov, Sergei — A scientist working in the Soviet Union's Biological warfare program

Smirnov, Vadim — Colonel in the Red Army

Kozlov, Nikolay — KGB officer

Kozlova, Svetlana — Kozlov's wife

Asadi, Mehdi — Iranian official in charge of Iran's CBW program

Mossad — Israeli foreign intelligence service

Ronan, Eitan — Mossad officer

Kidon — Mossad special operations unit

Shalev, David — Head of Mossad

Turmarkina, Sasha — Mossad officer

Smetanin, Volodya — Russian exile living in Paris

LeBrun, Mark — Mossad officer assigned to Paris

Mossberg, Michael — Mossad officer

Mojahedin (MEK) — People's Mojahedin Organization, or Mojahedin-e Khalq – militant Iranian anti-government group

Esfahani, Farhood — Iranian, Mossad asset

Esfahani, Seriya	Farhood's sister, Mossad asset
Bashur, Karzan	Mossad contact, member of PKK
PKK	Kurdistan Workers Party, militant nationalist organization
PDKI	Iranian offshoot of PKK
Gromov, Sergei	Ex-KGB officer, arms dealer
Bargouti, Khalid	Palestinian terrorist, head of the Palestinian Jihadist Army
PJA	Palestinian Jihadist Army
Hatimi, Adel	VEVAK (Iranian Intelligence) General

11 ***Behold, all they that were incensed against thee shall be ashamed and confounded: they shall be as nothing; and they that strive with thee shall perish.***

12 ***Thou shalt seek them, and shalt not find them, [even] them that contended with thee: they that war against thee shall be as nothing, and as a thing of nought.***

Old Testament
Book of Isaiah

"As a matter of policy, the State of Israel neither acknowledges nor denies any involvement in overseas assassinations. When asked, government ministers and intelligence chiefs might opine that the world was better off, but would never publicly admit culpability even as specifics were often leaked to the Israeli press in intimate details ... (Assassinations are often attributed to) *Israel's foreign intelligence service, in particular its elite special operations unit known as Kidon, or Spear. Although great secrecy shrouds the unit, it supposedly consists of a small group of men and women trained in combat, intelligence, and covert action."*

Darshan-Leitner, Nitsana. Harpoon: Inside the Covert War Against Terrorism's Money Masters (p. 38). Hachette Books. (Parentheses added)

SVERDLOVSK

... a host of invisible spoors barely more than a micron in diameter were borne downwind of the compound across adjoining Compound 32, a civilian residential area and a ceramics factory, and beyond.

CHAPTER 1

Yekaterinburg straddles the border between Europe and Asia where she presides serenely over the time-worn Urals. It's a pleasant place, easy on the eyes, lying in a plain with a small river, the Iset, running through its center. Picturesque and well-maintained embankments are built up all along the river where the inhabitants of the city enjoy promenades and picnics when the weather is mild. The residents are inordinately fond of their city.

Originally, the city was named after Peter the Great's wife, Yekaterina, and was one of Russia's first industrial centers. It was also the unfortunate venue for the grisly massacre of the last Russian Tsar, Nicholas Romanov. The Tsar, his wife Aleksandra and their five children, and four attendants were shot, bayoneted, and clubbed to death by Bolsheviks there on July 17, 1918, in the cellar of a house commandeered from a local merchant. The Church of the Blood stands on the spot today.

Winters are long and outlast their welcome well into April. But the snow begins to melt in March.

Today Yekaterinburg boasts a population of nearly one and a half million, but in 1979 it was only 350 thousand. In 1946 the Soviets renamed it Sverdlovsk and designated it a "closed city." Like ancient Peking's "Forbidden City," no foreign eyes were permitted there, not to protect the privileges of an emperor, but to protect certain activities the Soviets wished to conceal. This was likely the reason Gary Powers' U2 spy plane was there, above the city when it was shot down in 1960.

March 31, 1979 - Military Compound 19, Sverdlovsk, USSR

Under a lowering sky a winter rain froze immediately upon hitting any surface and coated the muddy ground leaving walkways and buildings covered in a thin skein of ice that transmitted the chill through the soles of one's shoes and made locomotion hazardous. Harsh gusts of wind made it hard to keep one's footing while passing between the various buildings that comprised Military Compound 19.

Milder spring weather had not yet arrived in the Urals. The snow that had covered the ground since the previous October had only just begun to melt, leaving muddy areas surrounding sad drifts of dirty snow that had now temporarily re-frozen. The edges of the drifts were nearly black with filth. As the snow retreated, the uncollected detritus and trash of the previous year were exposed like islets revealed by a retreating tide.

The snow was as yet unchallenged by thaw in the shade of the forests where it remained white in contrast with the city. On the horizon stood the pine-bedecked Utkusskiy Mountains, ancient peaks worn down by the ages, mere hills compared to the Caucasus. But they served inhabitants of the city of Sverdlovsk as a winter recreation area complete with a ski jump.

On this day at the end of March Sergeant Azamat Akhmetov sweated inside the uncomfortable, charcoal-lined hazmat suit that encased his entire body. The production laboratory in Compound 19 was climate controlled, but it didn't help. Akhmetov was removing a filter from the exhaust of one of the drying machines. During his daily inspection, the sergeant discovered the filter had become clogged. It was his job to remove it, have it cleaned and re-installed as quickly as possible. This required him to disassemble the filter housing, making certain the shut-off valve between the drying machine and the filter was closed first. Once removed, the filter had to be placed in an air-tight bag before it could be carried to the maintenance room. Akhmetov's hands were clumsy in his suit's thick, rubber gloves, and it took longer than anticipated to finish the job.

It was already late in the day, and he did not plan to re-install the filter until Monday. It was already late Saturday, and Sunday was a free day when he could escape into town from the military drabness of the barracks for some drinks and maybe a movie. He reasoned that everyone else but the poor saps that drew guard duty would be off, so with luck the repairs to the filter would not even begin until Monday morning.

Light was already dissolving into darkness by the time Akhmetov finished, and the mess hall would have begun serving hot food. He carried the encased filter to the maintenance room where the sergeant in charge received it with a sour face. "It's about time, Akhmetov. I'm starving." He, too, was anxious to get to his chow hall meal.

"I'll trade jobs with you any time," Akhmetov shot back. He scribbled a note reporting removal of the filter and stuck it in the supervisor's pigeonhole to report that the equipment was in the shop for repair, then turned to head for the decontamination room.

"Hey," said the maintenance sergeant. "You're supposed to make an entry in the logbook?"

He was right. An entry in the official logbook would show that Akhmetov had removed the filter, but he was exhausted and hungry. The decontamination procedure to remove the hazmat suit was time-consuming, and the chow hall would close in a half-hour. "The note for the shift supervisor is enough," he said. "I'll fill out the log book Monday morning."

Compound 19 occupied an area one kilometer square. It contained all the elements necessary to make it a self-contained city within a city, including a hospital and a crematory for the incineration of the remains of animals that had been test subjects. It was divided into a residential zone, a production zone with laboratories, vivisection facilities, and storage bunkers buried deep underground. The facility was protected by high walls topped with concertina wire.

Directly alongside was another facility of equal size, known as Compound 32 where elements of the 34th Motorized Rifle Division were stationed with the mission of protecting Compound 19 and other militarily significant installations. Officers lived with their families in one part of the compound while equipment storage and maintenance and barracks for common soldiers occupied the remaining area. From outside the walls, it was impossible to distinguish between the two special facilities.

Doctor Sergey Vinogradov sensed a nearly imperceptible fragrance in the air, the kind that hangs in one's nostrils in spring with promises of the coming warmth. But although the biting cold of winter had passed, spring would not truly arrive until the first of May when leaves would begin to reappear on the trees.

Vinogradov was the day supervisor of Compound 19's microbiological lab. He was always the first of the shift to arrive. As usual, he checked the logbook at the Duty Officer's post on Monday morning. The absence of any entry pleased him as it meant there was no impediment to the laboratory's operations.

Doctor Vinogradov was not one to fail to achieve the production quotas demanded by the Ministry of Defense and returned the lab to full operation as soon as his team was in place.

It was noon before he checked his pigeonhole and discovered Sergeant Akhmetov's note. The drying machines that separated the microscopic anthrax spoors from moisture and encased them in silicone had been running for over four hours without filtration. Doing his utmost to cover his panic Vinogradov rushed back to the lab and ordered the unfiltered equipment to be shut down.

Horrified, he called the repair shop and was told the filter had been cleaned and was ready for re-installation. Vinogradov ordered the work to be done immediately, and ninety minutes later the drying equipment was running again.

During the interval in which the equipment

operated without a filter, a host of invisible spoors barely more than a micron in diameter were borne downwind of the compound across adjoining Compound 32, a civilian residential area and a ceramics factory, and beyond.

If he were not such a good microbiologist Doctor Vinogradov would not have been working at Military Compound 19 under the auspices of the Soviet Union's cloaked biological warfare program. The aim of Vinogradov's program at Military Compound 19 was to develop *Bacillus antrhacis* into a biological weapon, specifically to create a usable aerosol version that could be weaponized. Current thinking was to incorporate it into a warhead for the SS-18 ICBM. He was working with a strain of the disease dubbed Anthrax 836, and it was the most powerful strain in existence anywhere on earth.

So-called "special institutes" like Compound 19 were created all over the USSR, and each of them worked on the development of a different microbial strain: at the Sverdlovsk institute it was anthrax – the so-called *Sibirskaya Yazva*, at Kirov it was the plague, and at Podolskiy it was tularemia.

CHAPTER 2

Sverdlovsk, 1979

Colonel Vadim Smirnov was in a hurry to return to Sverdlovsk. His official visit to Perm had been interrupted the day before, 2 April, by an urgent call from the Duty Officer of Compound 32.

"Something terrible is happening, sir. People are dying, and they've called many generals and other senior officers from the District to investigate. They're inspecting the mess hall and all the barracks – the whole compound. Ambulances are being called at every hour to take away those who've fallen ill."

Colonel Smirnov immediately contacted the Division Medical Officer who confirmed that 12 people already were dead, including Warrant Officer Rogov, the officer in charge of supplies. Rogov had been among the first to die. "For some unknown reason they've delayed an autopsy, but I can tell you, Rogov's body looked as though he'd been terribly beaten," the Medical Officer told him.

"You mean he was attacked?" Smirnov had a hard time believing such a thing could happen in his command.

"No, no, of course not. It's just that he was covered in bruises. His wife said he had fallen suddenly ill with the flu to the point where he could no longer breathe."

Full of dread, Smirnov drove into the compound at eight AM on the 3rd of April and found on his desk an official list showing the ranks and other personal data of the military and civilians employed at the Compound who had died or fallen ill. By then fourteen had died and another twenty-five had been taken away by ambulance. He ordered that the Compound be sealed immediately and guards posted inside and outside the perimeter.

In short order, reserves were called in from around the *Oblast[1]* to help contain and investigate the situation, and daily general meetings were initiated. At the first of these, the District Commanding Officer fixed his gaze on Colonel Smirnov and said, "People are dropping dead all over Compound 32, but the Divisional Commander tells me nothing."

The criticism stung. Smirnov had returned to his command only hours earlier and the District Commander had been there since the day before. All the ill and deceased had complained of trouble breathing. All the affected personnel had eaten in the mess, and initial suspicions centered on food preparation, specifically under-cooked meat, dairy products, and canned goods. The traditional Russian greeting kiss was forbidden, to be replaced with a handshake. All fatalities were to be reported immediately to Division Headquarters.

---

[1] Political region

Afterwards in his office Smirnov confronted the Commander. "You've obviously concluded that we're dealing with an outbreak of anthrax." The disease, he knew, could be contracted from infected meat and other products from infected animals.

The Commander fell into a chair, worry sagging his face. "By all accounts, we are dealing with anthrax. Every possible measure to contain the infection must be taken." He exhaled heavily. "And then we must consider what can be said publicly. Several of the dead lived in town, and word will spread rapidly. We have to avoid a general panic."

It was still mid-morning, and Smirnov called his wife to let her know he had returned. She worked as a doctor in an *internat* (orphanage) less than a kilometer from Compound 32. He could tell by her voice that something was very wrong. "What is it? Why are you so upset?"

She was near tears. "All the children here are sick. They're all coughing and have high temperatures. Some are vomiting and have diarrhea. She was instituting a quarantine. The blood froze in Smirnov's veins.

The spread of the infection outside the Compound suggested that the Division mess was not the source of the infection. Nevertheless, over the following three days the mess was subjected to an exhaustive search by regional sanitary inspectors. Not a single knife or fork was excluded, and in the end, nothing could be found.

The next day Colonel Smirnov called a general meeting in the officers' club of all Compound residents, nearly three thousand profoundly frightened people. By then 33 sick people had been taken away by ambulance. "We are taking all necessary steps to insure the rapid transport of the sick to hospitals. We're also setting up a system to care for children left alone. There will be regular patrols of all living quarters, so please leave your doors unlocked. Don't open your windows or vents. And don't be upset that an officer will enter your apartments every half-hour to check for illness."

Residents were permitted to leave the Compound only with passes, and external communications with the city were shut down. Sites for the incineration of all meat were set up, and strict rationing of remaining stores was introduced.

There were no questions.

Regardless of Smirnov's efforts to limit knowledge of the disaster, rumors of massive casualties among military personnel spread throughout Sverdlovsk. The conscripts told their wives, their wives told their friends, and of course the entire Party apparatus of the *oblast* knew about it. And the retelling exaggerated the level of the problem with some saying that unclaimed bodies lay in the roads.

Worst of all for Colonel Smirnov were unfounded allegations that his troops were responsible for the outbreak. Even Boris Yeltsin, then First Secretary of the Regional *Oblast* Committee declared that the Division was responsible for the deaths. This prompted the outraged Colonel to contact Moscow and demand that Yeltsin be told the truth.

Doctor Vinogradov had not been derelict in his duty. Immediately upon discovering the lapse of security at his lab, he informed the commander of Compound 19 who in turn contacted the highest authorities of the Ministry of Defense and *Biopreparat*[2]. Besides the gravity of the situation in Sverdlovsk, every Soviet official was aware that the USSR was a signatory of the Biological Weapons Convention of 1972. But under cover of its "closed cities" the Soviet Union continued to develop bio-weapons without pausing its stride. The Sverdlovsk incident threatened to disclose the Kremlin's deceit to the world.

On 4 April, Colonel Smirnov received an order to report to the District Commander at the command building of Compound 19. He was met at the gate by security and escorted into Zone 3 to a building that was no more than 200 meters from the quarters he shared with his wife in the neighboring compound.

He found the District Commander waiting for him accompanied by three men, one of whom was in mufti with a star on his lapel which identified him as a Hero of the Soviet Union. The other two strangers wore white coats.

"Colonel Smirnov," said the District Commander without bothering with introductions. "I want you to look at this." He swept his arm over two maps spread out across a large table. One was a large-scale map of the city of Sverdlovsk.

Pointing to the second, smaller scale map, the District Commander pointed out the locations of livestock burial sites throughout the *Oblast*. But it was the proliferation of red crosses marked on the map that caught Smirnov's attention.

Catching his glance, the Commander said, "The red crosses mark the spots where fatalities have

---

[2] Биопрепарат, "Biological substance preparation"

occurred." He picked up a list and handed it to Smirnov. "This is a list of the dead. We have 36 so far."

The man in mufti interrupted them. With an annoyed glance at the District Commander, he said, "I suppose I'll have to introduce myself. I'm Chaikov, Chief of the 15th Directorate of the General Staff of the USSR. We are extremely concerned, Colonel Smirnov, by reports that Military Compound 32 is constantly penetrated by unauthorized personnel who collect samples of the air and the snow and climb onto the roofs of the living quarters. This is what we hear in Moscow, Colonel Smirnov, and we take it very seriously." He pointed an accusatory finger at the astounded Colonel.

Smirnov was taken aback by the accusatory tone. "I live in Compound 32," he said with more vehemence than might have been prudent. "It's been three days since I sealed the compound and introduced a strict admittance regime. I organized guards for the compound, both inside and outside the walls. No suspicious people got into the compound, no one took air or snow samples, and no one climbed to the roofs. There is, however, a road that passes between the two compounds that is open to all inhabitants of the city."

One of the men in white coats interrupted rudely, "You don't have all the facts, Colonel."

Adopting a tone to match, Smirnov turned to face him and said with considerable heat, "I'm the Division Commander, the senior officer in the compound, and I'll bear full responsibility for my words and actions. And I'm proud of the way my people have conducted themselves during this crisis. Some of my officers live in the city and must ride the trolley to work. The trolleys are always full, but if someone in uniform comes aboard, everyone else leaves the car at the next stop. If there are, as you say, facts of which I've not been made aware, then I strongly suggest you share them with me immediately if it means saving lives.

"The Party needs to take steps to prevent more deaths instead of looking for scapegoats. I've never seen such incompetence. We need medicines and food, not rhetoric."

(Defense Minister Ustinov and General Secretary Brezhnev were quickly brought up to date on Sverdlovsk. But already by the second day word of the incident had leaked to the West, and the Kremlin scrambled to stay ahead of the rumors.)

Colonel Smirnov was gratified when a short time later Moscow ordered that tetracycline tablets be provided to all his personnel. But only one batch arrived, enough only for the officers who made the rounds of the apartments and houses where people had fallen ill. It took several more days for a supply sufficient for everyone to be sent to them.

On 5 April the Chief Medical Officer of the Ministry of Defense, Petr Buranov arrived in Sverdlovsk with a group of epidemiologists. Smirnov opined that they were already aware of what had really happened. After a tour of Compound 32, one of the visitors asked Smirnov to order his officers and enlisted men to write reports showing that their wives had purchased meat at non-official markets. Smirnov refused to give such an order. He guessed immediately that the visitors' only task was to deflect suspicion away from Military Compound 19 to conceal the true reason for the deaths.

A few days later, Colonel Smirnov paid a visit to

the *Voyentorg*[3] and ran into his old friend, Raisa Petrovna, who ran the place. He accepted her invitation to coffee, and they sat in a quiet corner. It was obvious that Raisa had something on her mind.

He lit a cigarette and exhaled. "Well, out with it, Raisa. You're bursting to tell me something."

She leaned toward him and said in a hoarse whisper, "Vadim Aleksandrovich, do you know what they're doing with the bodies?"

"I think they're being quarantined in the morgues," he replied.

"Not at all. They're taking the coffins from the morgues without the consent of the families and loading them onto flatbed trucks. They select one member of the deceased's family, mother, father, or wife, and put them on the trucks with the coffins. The trucks are accompanied by a couple of militia cars to the cemetery. But the cops won't go past the cemetery gates. The trucks carry the coffins and family members to open graves, and the family members are left to unload and bury the coffins by themselves."

Colonel Smirnov was incensed, but there was nothing he could do in the face of the Soviet government's measures to organize a cover-up.

---

[3] Voyentorg (военторг) – a sort of Post Exchange (PX).

Colonel Smirnov was not alone in his frustration. The afternoon of 4 April Margarita Ilyenko,[4] chief physician at Sverdlovsk's Hospital No. 24 in the city's southern district, received a telephone call at home from a colleague at another hospital. Skipping the formalities, he asked, "Do you have any patients who are dying?"

Of course, there were mortalities in every hospital, but it was apparent that something out of the ordinary was happening. "Yes," she replied, "Why do you ask?"

"We've had several patients exhibiting high fevers, coughing, headaches, and vomiting accompanied by chills and chest pains. They died very quickly."

"Is it some sort of flu?"

"The symptoms are similar, but we're not sure. And there are reports of more people coming into clinics with the same complaints."

Earlier in the day, Doctor Ilyenko had been horrified when she made her rounds. She found the living and the dead lying together. All were listed as suffering from pneumonia or influenza.

Over the next two days five more people died at Ilyenko's hospital. As the death toll mounted, autopsies revealed a terrible truth: anthrax bacteria were found in the lungs and lymph nodes of the victims. Despite official announcements that the infection was caused by tainted meat, Ilyenko and the pathologists could conclude only that it had been carried through the air,

---

[4] This account is based on "A Puzzle of Epidemic Proportions" By David Hoffman, Washington Post Foreign Service, December 16, 1998.

not by contaminated meat. Despite their conviction, no one dared contradict the official pronouncements.

An emergency committee was organized to deal with the crisis, headed by officials sent from Moscow. Hospitals were disinfected and houses in the Chkalovskiy district were washed down with chlorine.

Dozens of autopsies showed sharp hemorrhaging of the lungs and lymph nodes, clear evidence of an airborne infection. But the KGB seized every autopsy report. Top Soviet infectious disease expert Vladimir Nikiforov was dispatched from Moscow to supervise all pathological work, and he made certain that everyone hewed to the tainted meat line.

Before it was over 50,000 people were temporarily evacuated to camps set up and guarded by the military. Over 100 people died and many more were infected. Finally, the central authorities supplied sufficient vaccine to treat the population.

CHAPTER 3

1985

A perceptive person might have read pity in the *Rezident's* face. He was speaking to an officer he genuinely liked and who might have had a brilliant future.

"You will leave on the first plane to Moscow in the morning. Neither of you will be permitted to leave Embassy premises, and you will be escorted to the airport."

It would have been difficult to read Captain Nikolay Kozlov's face. He sat in stony silence next to his equally silent wife, Svetlana, whose expression alternated between despair and obstinacy. Inwardly, he was furious at the foolish, spoiled woman. She was a beauty, for sure, a spoiled, pampered daughter of the Nomenklatura.

Svetlana had pursued him shamelessly when he was a young, handsome KGB lieutenant on the way up the ladder. But now he suspected the attraction had been only physical. Nikolay with his movie star good looks made a fitting accoutrement that she enjoyed showing off to her friends. Her father, a high Communist Party official in the Moscow city government, approved of the match. KGB officers were politically reliable, after all.

That his wife was shallow and self-centered, Nikolay put down to her upbringing among the red-starred glitterati of the capital. He had to admit he'd enjoyed the attention at first, especially the nice, two-room apartment on *Kutuzovskiy Prospekt* that her father arranged after the marriage. Svetlana's father's influence also moved him up the list for a plum foreign assignment. Everyone knew this, and he felt slightly ashamed of being put ahead of his peers, but the idea of living abroad, especially in Paris, was irresistible. At heart he was a romantic, and Paris was the most romantic place on earth.

Svetlana had been excited. She imagined a fine apartment in a good neighborhood and shopping to her heart's content. She chattered constantly about her expectations with her friends and actually worked hard to learn French. She pictured herself and Nikolay strolling arm in arm down the Champs Elysees and popping into expensive dress shops.

Her excitement continued right up until the moment they were shown to their Embassy quarters on *Boulevard Suchet*. This was in the 16th Arrondisement, the richest section of Paris. But as a lieutenant he was assigned to a communal apartment with three other families with whom they shared a kitchen and toilet. Evidently, Svetlana's father's influence did not extend all the way to Paris.

Despite an increasingly unhappy home life, Nikolay excelled at his job. He was under cover as a junior Novosti correspondent which gave him access to a broad swath of Parisians. His fluent French, good looks, and naturally sophisticated manner made him attractive to the French. He played the cosmopolitan well and soon had a string of sources that Moscow valued. After a year he was promoted to the rank of Captain.

Along with the promotion came the promise of better living quarters, but the waiting list was long. Svetlana's constant complaining frequently drove him out of the apartment, leaving her alone to stew. Looking back, he could see the inevitability of her straying, and he shouldered his share of blame.

He'd done his best to improve her mood. Whenever possible he brought her to receptions or dinner parties. At one of these they were introduced to a handsome young Frenchman named Remy Blanchard from the Foreign Ministry Press Office. Blanchard seemed anxious to develop a relationship with them, and Nikolay thought he made a good recruitment target.

Svetlana liked Blanchard and appreciated his many kindnesses. Apparently well-off, the Frenchman often invited them to dine at expensive restaurants and always picked up the tab.

Nikolay learned that his wife was sneaking out of the Russian diplomatic compound alone, ignoring the rule that wives were to be in pairs or otherwise accompanied whenever they ventured off Embassy premises. At first, he attributed this to Svetlana's belief that "rules were for other people." He tried to reason with her, and she became defensive and cagy, refusing to tell him where she went on these outings. As incredible as it seemed, he suspected there was another man. Then one day, she disappeared for good. The entire Embassy security staff set out to find her.

Strangely enough, the only person he could turn to was an American intelligence officer with whom he had been in contact for some time. For some reason he trusted this man. He fully expected a recruitment attempt, and if his wife had defected he thought he might accept. But it didn't turn out that way.

His friend confirmed that Svetlana had fallen into a French honey trap. It didn't work out for either the French or Svetlana who could not believe the man she'd been sleeping with was more interested in what she could tell him about Soviet codes than he was in her. She knew nothing about codes, which disappointed the French, who dumped her back onto the street.

Eventually, Svetlana made her way back to the Embassy, but it was too late, both for her and Nikolay. The American, as expected, offered recruitment or defection, but Nikolay refused. No matter what, he would not be branded a traitor, and his friend did not press him, but suggested that should he ever need a friend, he would be there. He gave Nikolay a rudimentary contact plan to use in Moscow, but he threw it away before he returned to the Embassy.

The die had been cast. There was no option but to share his wife's disgrace. And now they sat next to one another on an Aeroflot flight to Moscow. God alone, if he existed, knew what awaited them.

CHAPTER 4

Of course, Svetlana was clever enough not to tell the whole truth when she came back. She admitted to an illicit love affair but failed to mention that French intelligence had pitched her. Under the circumstances, Nikolay did nothing to contradict her.

Nevertheless, the affair left an indelible black mark on his record. He was called before a board of inquiry at the Lubyanka and admonished for failing to control his wife and not reporting her behavior. Fortunately, the colonel who presided over the board had a good opinion of Nikolay, whose operational record was excellent.

They gave him a job in the French Section at FCD Headquarters at Yasenevo where he knew he would languish forever. He would never again be promoted, and he would never be given another overseas assignment.

Svetlana immediately moved back with her family, and she never saw him again. It was possible that her father felt some guilt for his daughter's conduct and its effect on Nikolay's career, so he still had the apartment on *Kutuzovskiy Prospekt*.

Occasionally he would be called upon to escort French visitors and ply them with assertions of the superiority of the Soviet system. But Moscow's opulent operas and ballet, fine meals in restaurants closed to normal citizens, and the spectacle of Red Square at night paled in his own mind in comparison with what he had seen of France. As the corrupt, Brezhnev era ground on, Nikolay felt less and less like a patriot.

One place in Moscow that might rise to Parisian standards was the Aragvi Restaurant on *Tverskaya Ulitsa*. It was literally the only place in the capital where Georgian cuisine could be obtained and had been a favorite of Lavrenti Beria and a hang-out for movie stars, the Nomenklatura, and the KGB.

"Do you see that old man over against the wall?" The question was asked by Nikolay's friend Stanislav Bukovskiy. The occasion was a celebratory meal in honor of Bukovskiy's upcoming assignment as *Rezident* in Belgium.

Nikolay looked in the direction indicated and spotted a thin old man in worn tweeds thirstily downing a goblet of Georgian wine. Bukovskiy whispered, "That's Kim Philby."

"He doesn't look well," said Nikolay.

"Whisky is killing him," replied Bukovskiy. "He's doesn't have much longer, I think." He tucked into his *lobio*, a Georgian bean dish. "Nobody trusts him, anyway, the old fucker."

The waiter served a round of chicken in garlic walnut sauce, and everyone helped themselves to another shot of ice cold vodka, anxious to down as much as they could before the wine was served. There were a dozen officers at the table, all from the French and Benelux sections. Bukovskiy and Nikolay sat side by side, a sign of Bukovskiy's affection for the ill-starred officer.

As everyone tucked into their meal, Bukovskiy

whispered, "Kolya,[5] I wish I could take you with me to Brussels. Everyone knows you are an excellent officer. It's a tragedy what happened." He sighed and sipped his wine. "But there's nothing to be done. You're just running in place here in Moscow, like a gerbil on a wheel, and I hate to see it. May I make a suggestion?"

"Of course," replied Nikolay. He groaned inwardly. Friends were always patronizing him, and he hated being the subject of sympathy.

"There is no future for you in the First Chief Directorate," continued Bukovskiy. "You must know this. Another foreign assignment is out of the question. Therefore, may I suggest you consider transferring to a position where foreign assignments are not so important? It might give you a chance at another promotion."

"What do you mean?"

"Transfer to the Second Chief Directorate."

"Counterintelligence and security?"

"That's right. Listen, I have a good comrade over there. He can make sure your application is accepted and find an assignment somewhere far from the capital. You're not doing yourself any favors remaining at the Center in the FCD where everyone knows what happened. It's a dead-end, and you're better than that."

---

[5] The diminutive of Nikolay

CHAPTER 5

Sverdlovsk, December 1991

The flight from Moscow had been uneventful and not especially comfortable in the Antonov-32, and Mehdi Asadi's mood could not have been described as sunny when they landed finally at Koltsovo Airport. A chill Ural wind invaded the passenger cabin as soon as the hatch was opened. He pulled his heavy coat more tightly around him and went down the stairs onto the tarmac. Snow had been bulldozed and stood in dirty piles at the sides of the runways. It was a clear winter's day with a light-blue sky arching overhead. In the distance a range of low mountains marched across the horizon. In the Iranian's opinion, it was an entirely unremarkable landscape.

Asadi's traveling companion, Colonel Arkadiy Zhukov of the KGB, was dour and uncommunicative. He had uttered not a word during the achingly slow flight, sitting across the aisle hunched in his greatcoat. This had not bothered Asadi, at all. Yes, the Russians were godless infidels, but they were useful to the Supreme Leader and the Ministry of Intelligence and Security, so he would tolerate them. Technology supplied by the Soviets was key to the Islamic

Republic's nuclear development program, and KGB training had made Iran's intelligence service more effective. The present task was to take advantage of their ally's current political deterioration.

Mehdi Asadi was a pharmacologist and scientific advisor to the President of Iran. For many years there had been exchanges of scientific information with the Soviets. Now he was under the direct orders of Brigadier General Mohammed Rezaei whose brief was to recruit useful foreigners to Iran's cause. It was important to move quickly before every institution of the Soviet state collapsed.

A heavy ZIL sedan waited for them outside the terminal and carried them to the center of Sverdlovsk. Neither man spoke during the journey, each wrapped in his own thoughts. The car pulled to a stop at a two-story red brick building with a large, metal door at one end. It was on a broad avenue inevitably called *Prospekt Lenina.* To Asadi's eye the building must have been pre-revolutionary to judge from the ornate brickwork. A brass sign affixed to the wall beside the door announced that this was the KGB Administration for the Central Military Region.

Inside, they were greeted by a handsome, young-looking officer in uniform who introduced himself as Major Nikolay Kozlov. The major had an elegant look about him and projected an image of insouciance though not studiously so, which led Asadi to conclude that it was a natural trait. He had slightly too long light brown hair and a thin moustache. Kozlov conducted them to a conference room where an older military officer waited. Bottles of mineral water and fruit juice along with biscuits and fruit had been placed around the table. Kozlov introduced the older officer as Colonel Smirnov, commanding officer of the local garrison.

Kozlov was curious about the reason for the hastily arranged visit of the foreign visitor. The Iranian was of average height with a spare frame and a narrow face with prominent cheek bones over a neatly trimmed beard. Beneath his heavy coat he wore a dark suit and a white collarless shirt buttoned at the throat, but no tie. At first sight he did not appear to be the sort of person who smiled very much, and he exuded a mysterious, not quite unpleasant odor like the spices at an exotic bazaar mixed with sweat.

Introductions completed, Zhukov got right down to business. The agreed language was English which everyone spoke well except for Colonel Smirnov whose comprehension was basic. "Our Iranian colleague, Dr. Asadi, is to meet with senior personnel from Compound 19. You," he glowered at Kozlov and Smirnov, "are to facilitate these meetings with all due dispatch. We return to Moscow the day after tomorrow, so you have an entire day to get it all done. Give it your top priority."

"You wish us to take him inside Compound 19?" asked Smirnov, somewhat taken aback. Sverdlovsk itself was a city forbidden to foreigners, and Compound 19 was its most sensitive installation.

Zhukov was uncomfortable with the question and cast a sidelong glance at Asadi. He rubbed his jaw and replied, "The meetings are to take place here in this building."

Zhukov and the others remained in the conference room after Asadi was sent to a KGB safehouse where he was to remain out of sight until the next day. The Moscow Center officer slumped in his chair, lit a cigarette, and wearily shook his head as the door closed behind the Iranian. Relieved to be speaking Russian, he said, "I know this is quite unusual, but the orders from the Center are clear. Things are changing rapidly in Moscow after the coup attempt, and the word is that the KGB will be disbanded and reorganized in the very near future thanks to Kryuchkov's involvement.[6] That's the reason for the haste. We must do our best to organize for the future while we still can. There's no telling who'll be purged."

Kozlov was shocked. "Disband the KGB?" Such a thought had never occurred to him, or to any other Soviet citizen for that matter.

"Oh," said Zhukov with a wave of his hand, "we'll still be around, but it looks like they intend to break us up into different organizations, foreign intelligence and internal security. Kryuchkov scared the shit out of them when he tried to take out Gorbachev."

Kozlov persisted. "What do you mean 'organize for the future?' Organize for what?"

Zhukov looked at him like a teacher might look at a backward student. "What do you think, Major? We must safeguard the security of the Motherland. These idiots taking power in Moscow now will destroy the country even more than that bumbling idiot Gorbachev. We have to position ourselves to take it back when the time comes."

"And how do the Iranians fit in?" asked Smirnov whose face was set in stone. Long years of practice enabled him to present an impassive façade regardless

---

[6] KGB Chairman Vladimir Kryuchkov was the leader of a coup attempt against President Mikhail Gorbachev in August 1991.

of what he was thinking.

"We're holding onto alliances that will be useful in the future. There's no guarantee that the work of Compound 19, of the entire *Biopreparat* complex will continue. The Iranians will pursue certain lines of research, which they will be prepared to share with us."

"But then the Iranians will know as much as we," protested Kozlov. "Can we trust the Muslims?"

Smirnov, who had spent a few years in Afghanistan before returning to Sverdlovsk, was especially interested in Zhukov's answer. The war experience had not resulted in an elevation in rank for Smirnov, but he had gained a new appreciation for a relatively quiet life in the Urals.

The Moscow Center officer was no happier with the arrangement, but he had his orders. "We have few friends in the world and little choice. We'll make sure that whoever agrees to work in Iran remains loyal to us. They wouldn't be working where they are now unless they were loyal. It's a chance we have to take in such desperate times."

It was getting late in the afternoon, and darkness still fell early this time of year. Kozlov had arranged for Zhukov to be put up in the KGB guesthouse. After the weary Moscow Center officer left, Kozlov and Smirnov decided they needed a drink or two and headed for the *Tsentralniy* Hotel on Malysheva Street. Unspoken was the fact that both felt more comfortable talking outside the precincts of KGB Headquarters.

The *Tsentralniy* is a huge, Soviet-style hotel in the center of the city. It boasts a nice bar in the lobby and a decent restaurant that for an unknown reason is named the Savoy. Their uniforms guaranteed them a decent table and immediate service, and soon they had an iced bottle of vodka and a selection of *zakuski* on the table between them.

The two officers knew one another well – well enough to be honest. Kozlov had been in Sverdlovsk since 1987. At that time, Smirnov was still in Afghanistan, and though there had been no promotion, his service was recognized, and when he'd requested re-assignment back to his old command in Sverdlovsk, there had been no objection. All he wanted was a quiet life.

Kozlov poured them each a shot of vodka and raised his glass in salute, which Smirnov reciprocated. The first drink consumed, Kozlov poured them another. "Well, Vadim, what do you think?"

"About what? The Iranian, what Zhukov said?"

Kozlov lit a cigarette and let the smoke trickle through his nostrils. "Everything, I guess. I'm just glad we're not in Moscow. The shit is hitting the fan there."

"Do you what to know what I really think? I don't believe Zhukov is legitimate. The way he was talking makes me think he and whoever he's working for are acting behind the scenes without official government permission. The USSR no longer exists, and God only knows what's going to happen. You heard what he said about disbanding the KGB. These guys are working on their own without any official backing. That's what I think."

Kozlov grew thoughtful and finished his second vodka. Smirnov was probably right, but what, if anything, could be done about it? He had no idea to whom he could report such suspicions. Moscow Center was a scene of chaos, and nobody could be sure of anything. They were in the midst of a cataclysm so unexpected, so far-reaching that no one could be trusted. "But Zhukov is here under direct orders from the Center," he said. "As far as we can know, his mission is officially sanctioned. There is no choice but to obey."

Smirnov threw back his vodka and held the glass out for a refill. "Yes. '... no choice but to obey.' That's the Soviet way, isn't it? But the Soviet Union is dead, buried under decades of mismanagement and corruption and thousands of young Russians dead under the snow in Afghanistan."

"So, what do you suggest, Vadim?"

"Me? There's not a damned thing I can do, nor you either, I suppose. We'll just sit back and watch it happen. There is no one we can turn to, no one we can trust."

"Is it such a bad thing to let these scientists go?"

"Nikolay, I was here in 1979. I saw firsthand what they were up to and what happens when it gets out of control. Just a small accident caused the deaths of hundreds – men, women, children, too. And now Zhukov's friends want to hand it over the Iranians, to religious fanatics? Does that sound like a good idea to you? God knows what they'll do with such a capability."

"Do you think the scientists will actually agree to go to Iran?"

"Who knows? They must be as confused and worried as the rest of us. There's literally nowhere for them to go, no jobs if their programs here are shut down. Desperate men do desperate things."

The colonel was right. And there wasn't a damned thing either of them could do about it. "Let's get drunk," he said.

Dr. Sergey Vinogradov was now the chief scientist at Compound 19. His specialty remained anthrax, but his administrative duties put him in charge of the entire complex. The call to appear at the regional KGB headquarters mystified and frightened him. Given recent events in Moscow the country could expect seismic changes to come. Everything he had done since first coming to Sverdlovsk had been perfectly legal, sanctioned by the State. But every researcher, scientist, and soldier at Compound 19 was aware that their work violated an important international treaty to which the Soviet Union had been a signatory. In the current topsy-turvy atmosphere it was not beyond imagining that some sort of retroactive punishment could be enacted.

Doing his best to remain calm he entered the red brick building on *Prospekt Lenina* where a uniformed officer with a KGB major's stars on his blue epaulets accompanied him to a conference room. Inside, the officer introduced him to a swarthy-complexioned man in a civilian suit, without doubt a foreigner.

"Dr. Vinogradov, this is Mr. Asadi, a representative of the Iranian government. He wants a chat with you."

Again, English was the *lingua franca*.

Vinogradov, more confused than ever, took a seat at the table opposite the Iranian.

"That will be all, Major Kozlov," said Asadi. "You may leave us alone."

With a frown, Kozlov left the room closing the

door behind him.

"Dr. Vinogradov, thank you for coming to see me. Do you know why you're here?"

"No."

The Iranian smiled showing small, white teeth, but no warmth. "I can understand your confusion, but I assure you all is well. I'm here to make you an offer, a very generous offer to come to Tehran and continue your research."

Astounded, Vinogradov said, "But that's impossible. I am not permitted to leave the country."

"Dr. Vinogradov, we are here in KGB headquarters, my presence here was facilitated by the KGB, and under their protection. I can assure you that you will encounter no difficulties if you accept my offer."

The idea of escaping the disorder in Russia was both frightening and attractive to Vinogradov. The Iranian's next words convinced him. "We are prepared to pay you five thousand dollars a month for your services for as long as you remain in Iran."

The salaries of Vinogradov and his colleages at Compound 19 seldom exceeded the equivalent of a few hundred dollars per month.

Kozlov had returned to his office and immediately switched on the listening device planted in the conference room. Asadi's next words chilled him.

"My country has enemies that wish to destroy us, Dr. Vinogradov, and we need every weapon possible at our disposal. And, believe me, once we have a weapon we will not hesitate to use it, first on the Israelis and then on their infidel masters, the Americans."

Vinogradov's mind was spinning, and he wasn't even listening. "How will I get to Tehran?" he asked.

Asadi smiled again. Vinogradov thought it made him look more sinister than friendly. There was no warmth in those dark brown, nearly black eyes. That will be arranged by Colonel Zhukov and his colleagues. But before we get to that, there are some details we need to cover. We will need your files, as well. Will it be difficult?"

"My 'cookbooks?' I don't see a problem. No one will ask me any questions. Even better, a seed culture of dried anthrax spores can be safely transported in a small, sealed plastic vial no larger than your fingernail. It could be concealed in a pack of cigarettes and remain completely undetectable."

Satisfied, Asadi nodded. "Excellent. When the time comes you will be contacted and provided with appropriate tickets and documentation. For the time being, say nothing to your colleagues and be prepared to move at a moment's notice."

"How long will I have to wait."

"A few weeks at most. It will take some time for Colonel Zhukov to set up an escape route and develop a cover story for your departure. Be patient."

EITAN & SASHA

She reached inside her handbag and felt the reassuring grip of the Beretta. She would use it that morning for the first time in a real operation, and she steeled her mind against self-doubt and the normal human abhorrence of taking another's life. Her targets were enemies in a deadly serious war, and sympathy for an enemy was unwise. She would rely on her training, which had been extensive and harrowing.

CHAPTER 6

Vienna, Austria – January 1992

The Embassy of Israel in Vienna is in a largely residential neighborhood in the north-western district of Währing. The building itself is unprepossessing, consisting of four stories of white stucco with a red tile roof and dormer windows on the top floor.

Behind one of the dormer windows is a small office. It is not particularly impressive or tidy. Facing the window is a wooden desk containing an electric typewriter, two telephones, and a framed photograph of a group of soldiers against a desert background. There is a safe with a combination lock beside the desk. A few chairs and occasional tables that once had been in more formal rooms of the Embassy and an old sofa that often served as a bed for the occupant completed the furnishing. On the wall was a large map of Vienna. A threadbare carpet covered the floor. The door was armored and had a combination lock. There were few visitors to the office. It was drafty in winter and too warm in summer, discomforts that the sole occupant bore stoically.

Eitan Ronan was the Mossad station chief in Vienna as well as the manager of the *Kidon* unit in

Buy Another Day

Western Europe. He was not a man to adorn his work space with personal souvenirs or any other indication of sentimentality. The photograph of him and the surviving members of his unit in the Egyptian desert taken in 1973 was the only exception. It reminded him of where he came from and how easily it could be lost. He never wanted to forget that his country's existence was a day-to-day struggle.

Ronan was a big man with a mane of unruly jet-black hair and an eternal five o'clock shadow. He was not tall, but he had the build of a wrestler and was not the sort of person one would be pleased to chance upon in a dark alley. He favored French cigarettes, Gauloises to be precise, that produced an acrid blue smoke that some found difficult to tolerate. He was secretly pleased with the assignment to Vienna because the city offered an unparalleled assortment of baked sweets that were his only weakness.

The room next to his office also boasted an armored door behind which lay the local Mossad communications center which was manned twenty-four hours a day.

On a day in mid-January he was puzzling over local press reports concerning the disappearance of a visiting Russian diplomat in Vienna. Traces from Tel Aviv said the man was affiliated with the KGB. Ronan wondered if the Americans had him. If he'd been their agent he would be far from Austria by now, likely holed up in a safehouse somewhere in Northern Virginia.

He'd finished a plate of *kaisershmarren* and a mug of dark, strong coffee, and lit his third Gauloise of the morning when the phone rang. It was the internal secure line. Exhaling a thick cloud of smoke, he lifted the receiver to his year. "Yes?"

"Eitan, you have a visitor." It was the receptionist downstairs in the lobby. The word "visitor" connoted a walk-in. Such people came to the embassy with surprising frequency to offer their assistance to Israel or provide information they believed was vital. Most of them proved worthless, many suffered from mental illness. But it was the Mossad's responsibility to interview them because once in a blue moon a walk-in possessed valuable information, and even more rarely occupied an official position that made it worthwhile to try to turn them into agents in place.

"I'll be right down," rumbled Ronan.

He crushed out the cigarette and swept some classified documents from the desk to shove them into the safe, closed it and twirled the dial before heading out of the office and down the creaking wooden stairs at the back of the building. On the ground floor he consulted briefly with the receptionist.

"What have we got?"

"He's a Russian, according to his papers." The receptionist handed over a passport that identified the "visitor" as Aleksandr Shevchenko from Leningrad. The walk-in would have been frisked by the armed security guard and escorted to a small conference room just off the lobby. The room was equipped with a CCTV camera and audio pick-ups. On the monitor Ronan saw that the Russian was well-dressed, his suit more smartly cut than might be expected. He was a handsome man with light brown hair worn stylishly long and a thin moustache adorning his upper lip.

Ronan studied the passport. He'd suspected for a moment that they might be dealing with the missing

Russian from the newspapers, but the name didn't match. Nevertheless, a Russian walk-in was rare enough to pique his interest. "Did he say anything?"

"Well," replied the receptionist, "he said right out that he wanted to speak with the Mossad. He doesn't seem to be a nutcase. He doesn't speak German, but his French and English are pretty good."

Ronan's French was not good, but passable. In a pinch he could use Russian, too. His English was good. With the passport still in his hands, he made his way to the conference room, entering by a rear door. He dismissed the guard and took a seat facing the Russian. "My name is Moshe," he said. "Why are you here?"

The Russian regarded Ronan with curiosity. "Are you from the Mossad?" he asked.

Ronan's expression didn't change. "Why are you here?" he repeated.

The Russian smiled and withdrew a pack of cigarettes from his jacket, Marlboros. "Do you mind if I smoke?"

"Go ahead. But I have no time to waste. Get to the point quickly."

The Russian was quite calm. His hands did not shake as he lit the cigarette and inhaled deeply. He was the physical opposite of Ronan – trim, fair, and graceful. He regarded the Israeli with penetrating blue eyes, seemed to make up his mind about something, and said, "You're Mossad without doubt. First, my name is not Shevchenko. The passport is an alias. My real name is Nikolay Kozlov, and I'm a major in the KGB currently assigned to Sverdlovsk. I have important information about a danger to your country."

Ronan was not impressed. "That's interesting, but it's a claim you can't back up."

"Of course, I can. For example, your name is Eitan Ronan. You were born in Israel in 1948 in a kibbutz near Haifa called *Gan Shmuel*, you fought with the IDF in the 1973 war and joined Mossad shortly thereafter. You've been the Chief here in Vienna for the last three years. In the past you've been associated with the *Metsada*[7], but now you are assigned to Collections. Your KGB file is quite thick."

Ronan struggled to contain his surprise. "That's impressive but irrelevant. Why are you here?"

"As I said, I have information concerning the security of your country. I at first thought to go to the Americans but decided your service could best put the information to use."

"Are you defecting?"

The Russian shook his head. "No, I'm a Russian, and I have no desire to leave my country."

"How did you get here?"

"I had an alias passport from a previous assignment. I flew to Moscow and from there to Prague. Then I drove to Vienna. I will return via the same route as soon as we're finished here."

"Does anyone else know what you're doing?"

Kozlov scrutinized him for a beat before answering. "Just one person, someone I trust implicitly."

"Very well, assuming what you say is true, what is this information you claim to have?"

---

[7] Special Operations – assassinations, sabotage, paramilitary and psychological operations.

"First, what do you know about Sverdlovsk?"

"Not much except that it's a closed city."

"Sverdlovsk is the home of two closed facilities, one is military, known as Compound 32. Of course, it has regional defense responsibilities, but its other function is to protect the second compound, which is adjacent. The second is civilian under the auspices of the Ministry of Defense and an organization called *Bioprepart* and is designated Compound 19. Its purpose is the development and manufacture of biological weapons. It is part of a completely illegal secret program. The current head of Compound 19 is Doctor Sergey Vinogradov. His specialty is anthrax."

Ronan was taking notes. "And why are you telling me this?"

"The recent upheavals in my country have resulted in uncertainty and fear among such people as Dr. Vinogradov. They don't know whether they will lose the only jobs they've ever had or are qualified for or if they will be prosecuted as criminals. They're all very aware that their programs are prohibited by international agreement. So, some of them would welcome a way out."

"A way out?"

"And Vinogradov has found one. He's been recruited by the Iranians to continue his research under their protection. And from what I heard, the Iranians' number one target for a biological attack is Israel. Vinogradov will be carrying seed organisms and research documents with him to Tehran. He will advance their program by many years."

Kozlov took a hit from his nearly finished cigarette. "I thought you should know."

Ronan was curious. "Why? Why did you want us to know?"

Kozlov withdrew another cigarette from his pack and lit it with an old Zippo lighter. "That's a good question. I gave it a lot of thought, but it boils down to this. Communism is dead. The Soviet Union is dead. I see no justification for the continuance of whatever plans they had in mind for biological weapons. Whatever emerges from the chaos, there will be new policies, hopefully quite different."

"Is Vinogradov already in Iran?"

"He was still in Sverdlovsk when I left three days ago and won't leave until I return there. But I think he'll be traveling soon. He'll have to before the support structure to get him out collapses – a secret network of unreformed KGB officers. They will take him to Moscow and send him off, but not directly to Tehran. His first stop will be Paris where he'll catch an Iran Air flight to his final destination."

"Will he use an alias for travel?"

Kozlov looked down at the table and spoke as if he were embarrassed by his knowledge. "Yes. It's in my office in my desk drawer right now. That's why he can't leave before I get back."

Kozlov held nothing back from the Israeli. He even handed over a black and white photo of Vinogradov from Sverdlovsk KGB files.

Back in his office Ronan traced Nikolay Kozlov through Tel Aviv and was rewarded by confirmation that such a person existed, was a suspected KGB officer who had last been posted to Paris. A photo accompanied the traces. There could be no doubt that the visitor was who he said he was.

Ronan had to talk to David Shalev.

CHAPTER 7

David Shalev worked in an unremarkable but heavily guarded building that sat on a low hill off the Ayalon Highway in the northern suburbs of Tel Aviv. The building had five stories. There was no plaque at the entrance to announce that this was the headquarters of the Institute for Intelligence and Special Operations, colloquially known as the Mossad, which simply means "the Institute."

Shalev was a veteran of all of Israel's wars, declared and undeclared from the war of independence to the capture of Adolph Eichmann, to the retribution meted out to the authors of the Munich Massacre. He had become powerful not because it was his desire, but because of his experience and the esteem in which he was held by a series of Prime Ministers. He had reached that point in life where it was difficult to tell his age and those who knew and respected him hoped he would go on forever. David Shalev was the Head of the Mossad, where he was universally called the *memuneh*, a term which may be translated not only as "boss," but which in religious parlance is an angel in charge of dreams whose purpose is to translate the will of God for Man. But God had very little to do with Shalev's job.

Shalev took Ronan's call on the secure line in his

third-floor office. He listened to the field man's description of his meeting with Kozlov. "And do you believe him, Eitan?"

"I can't imagine what the Russians would have to gain if this were a disinformation operation. Kozlov's bio checked out. He is KGB, or whatever they're calling themselves these days."

"What do you suggest we do?"

"Obviously, the first thing is to monitor all flights into Paris from Moscow. We know the alias the scientist will be using, and there may be a source who can supply the passenger manifests. We'll know when he is coming and could place a *Kidon* unit at the airport."

"You're thinking assassination?"

"We could attempt an abduction, but assassination is a more likely possibility. But if he doesn't leave the airport transit area, there is little we can do."

Ronan's reasoning was solid. His rough, bear-like exterior belied a keen intelligence.

"What about the materials he's supposed to be carrying?" asked Shalev.

"Supposedly quite safe so long as the packaging remains intact. We can expect him to have it concealed somewhere on his body, perhaps in a cigarette pack. If there are a lot of documents, they would be in his luggage."

"Who would you use from *Kidon*?"

"We have a man in Paris, and I could send Sasha Turmarkina from here. I would go, too. Three should be enough. It would be a good team."

Shalev preferred meticulously planned operations, actions taken only after months of preparation and training. But he had a quality every field operator desired in a chief – trust in his people. In return they trusted him, and push-back on his decisions was rare.

In this instance, there was little time, at all. An immediate decision was required. Iran was an intractable enemy which had sworn the destruction of the Israeli state. They controlled hostile forces that threatened Israel's frontiers – Hezbollah in the north and the Palestinians and Hamas in the south. They could be permitted no advantage however great the risk.

Shalev could picture in his mind Palestinians passing into Israel from Gaza carrying biological agents that were difficult if not impossible to detect. They might even infect themselves before coming over. Or Hezbollah could send rockets with biologically charged warheads. The consequences of such an attack would be devastating. How long? How long, he wondered, would men like me have to lie awake at night tormented by such visions? But that was his job – imagine the worst possible horror and devise ways to thwart it.

"Eitan," he sighed into the phone. "Are you sure you want Turmarkina? She's untested."

"We just assigned her to *Kidon*. She passed all the tests, and she has to get her feet wet sometime."

"I leave it up to you, my friend. I don't think there is much chance of success, but I authorize you to proceed. There is really no other choice, and at the very least, if the scientist does pass through Paris as your walk-in says, we will know he was telling the truth and find another way to deal with it."

CHAPTER 8

Sasha Turmarkina's parents immigrated to Israel from the Soviet Union when she was a young child. She'd been with the Mossad since completing IDF service. She was recruited and groomed by family friend Eitan Ronan, and recently joined the elite and highly secret *Kidon* unit. Intelligence operatives should be able to fade into the background – anything but attract attention. Now around thirty-five, with ash blond hair and hazel eyes, Sasha was almost too beautiful to be a field operative.

For this assignment, she had adopted conservative dark clothing and glasses with thick, black frames. She wore a shapeless winter coat and a knit cap pulled over her hair. She carried a small, leather satchel with a change of clothing – all she'd had time to pack before catching the first flight out of Vienna. If she needed more clothes, she would buy them. Ronan had driven to Munich where he boarded another flight using an alias.

As soon as she arrived in Paris she headed straight for an apartment at 13, Rue de Tournon, not far from the Luxembourg Gardens. This was the address for the rendezvous Ronan had given her before leaving Vienna, explaining that it was the address of a friend of the Mossad. "Friend" was the proper term. "Ally" would have served as well. He was by no means an agent or under David Shalev's authority, but they shared enemies and many other similarities.

When she emerged from the Metro at Saint Germain-des-Prés a chill drizzle that was nearly snow fell gently, making footing slippery and driving people indoors. An gloomy sky cast the buildings in shades of gray. *Welcome to the City of Light,* she thought. *This could be Vienna.* She pulled her coat tighter and walked the several blocks to her destination, making certain she was not followed.

She arrived promptly at 10:30 a.m., the time set by Ronan. Rue de Tournon is a short, narrow street, a southern extension of the Rue du Seine, leading south from the Boulevard St. Germain to the domed façade of the French *Senat* at the head of the Luxembourg Gardens. It is lined with small shops and apartment buildings of indeterminate age, some of them a few centuries old if the locals are to be believed.

Parked cars lined both sides of the street. She arrived at No. 13 where she found a set of heavy, wooden double doors painted a non-descript green that apparently opened into a porte-cochere. There was a shop on either side of the doors, and the upper stories consisted of rows of large windows with heavy wooden shutters also painted green. Almost immediately she spotted the heavy-set figure of Eitan Ronan approaching from the direction of the *Senat.* He wore a dark raincoat and an Ascot cap pulled low over his forehead.

In Sasha's mind, Eitan Ronan was a force of nature. He had been a part of her life since she was a child of thirteen.

On October 6, 1973 Egypt launched a surprise attack across the Suez Canal sending five infantry divisions and over 1,000 tanks into the Sinai. Simultaneously, the Syrians attacked the Golan Heights in the north. The Egyptians controlled most of the East Bank within just a few days. It took a week before the Israelis could launch a counter-attack. By October 16 an Israeli force under the command of Ariel Sharon had crossed the canal but were met by stiff resistance at an Egyptian experimental agricultural station that dominated the key roads in the area. The initial Israeli forces were decimated.

The fighting was furious and involved hundreds of armored units, including a handful of half-track vehicles the Israelis had managed to get across with a few tanks. Israeli paratroops eventually were sent in, including a unit commanded by Captain Eitan Ronan. The unit soon faced annihilation by superior Egyptian forces and were under withering rocket and machine gun fire when one of the half-track drivers placed his vehicle in front of the unit, giving them enough time to escape. The driver of that half-track was Sasha's father, who was killed outright.

The first time she saw Ronan was when he arrived at the door of the Turmarkin apartment in Tel Aviv to deliver the news of her father's heroic death. From that moment on, Eitan Ronan had been a permanent fixture in her life, a surrogate father whom she sought to emulate.

Ronan reached her within a few seconds and patted her on the shoulder. "Good girl," he rumbled, "Right on time."

"I was trained by the best," she smiled.

"Well, let's go in so I can introduce you to the most interesting man in Paris."

He rang the buzzer beside the double doors, and a deep voice responded from the speaker. "*Qui est là ?*"

"Volodya, *c'est moi, Eitan,*" said Ronan, "*Puis je vous voir ?*" Ronan's French was mispronounced, but understandable and apparently recognizable, to judge from the response, which came in English.

"Eitan! Of course, come on up." Their unseen host buzzed the door open and with a final survey of the street, they entered and climbed the stairs to the third floor where an older man waited with the apartment door open. He embraced Ronan.

Their host was a somewhat rotund gentleman of advanced age with a fringe of white hair surrounding a bald pate. His skin was pale with slightly ruddy cheeks. He welcomed them with a warm smile.

"Eitan," he said, "It's so good to see you again. How are things in Vienna?" He gave Sasha a curious, but welcoming look and raised his eyebrows toward Ronan.

"Volodya," said Ronan, "this is Sasha Turmarkina, one of my most reliable people. Sasha, meet Volodya Smetanin, the most interesting man in Paris and a good friend of ours."

Smetanin took their damp coats and hung them on the *porte-manteaux* beside the door before inviting them into the living room. Sasha was curious about why Ronan considered him "the most interesting man in Paris." He was not tall, and he was obviously well over sixty. He looked soft, with sparkling blue eyes. He wore a pair of baggy corduroy trousers and a wool sweater over a white shirt. On his feet were *tufli* – Russian slippers.

"Please," he said, "sit. I'll bring us some hot tea and sweets. We need to warm you up."

Before they could say anything, he'd bustled off to the kitchen leaving them in a room filled with a multitude of objects that defined Smetanin's history. The walls were adorned with numerous photos and paintings with Russian subjects. A huge, brass samovar stood on a table in one corner. Above the doors leading to the dining room hung a dagger placed in a frame, with the point of the blade down, like a cross in an icon. It was one of the most unusual rooms Sasha had ever seen, but its distinct Russianness lent her a sense of comfort and familiarity.

The amiable physical appearance of their host belied the fact that Volodya Smetanin was a vital, industrious person, and this apartment was the center of a network of ratlines and informants that led deep inside Russia. Smetanin looked like everybody's jolly, favorite uncle, and his manners were those of another century. But behind this façade abided a ferociously keen mind fixated on tearing the bloody Bolshevik hands away from the throat of his beloved Russia. He had found many allies throughout his long struggle, including the Mossad.

He returned carrying a tray with a teapot, three china cups and saucers, and a plate of sweets. He set a cup before each of them and carefully poured the black, Russian tea. Ronan, who could never resist sweets, already had stuffed a chocolate cookie into his mouth.

Smetanin settled into a chair and sipped his tea. "It's been too long, Eitan. May I assume there is something I might be able to do for you and the young lady?"

Ronan popped a miniature *éclair* into his mouth and talked as he chewed. "Well, my old friend, I'm afraid I can't stay long. There are some arrangements I must make around town, but Sasha can fill you in after I leave. I just wanted you two to meet and get acquainted." With a glance at Smetanin, he said, "We do need a little help."

Sasha and Smetanin returned to their seats and tea after Ronan left and sipped the hot tea. Sasha asked, "How did you happen to come to Paris? It must be an interesting story."

"Well," he said, "interesting is the right word for it, I suppose, like the Chinese curse. It's a long and complicated story. Maybe I'll tell you about it sometime."

The rain had started again and drummed lightly against the windows.

"I'm sorry our weather is not more welcoming," said Smetanin. "I should offer you a cognac."

"Not even you can control the weather, *Gospodin*[8] Smetanin," said Sasha with a smile. "And no thanks on the brandy. As Eitan said, we need your help."

Time was of the essence now if they were to be successful tracking the Russian scientist and his deadly baggage.

With a regretful glance toward the bottle of cognac atop an old writing desk, he cocked his head to the side. "Tell me," he said, "and please call me Volodya."

---

[8] An old Russian term of respect corresponding to 'Mister.'

"That's very kind of you," she said, and then told him they needed access to the passenger manifests of all flights incoming from Moscow beginning immediately. There would be a certain passenger on one of those flights of great interest to the Mossad.

"You can't rely on your own people in Paris for this information?"

"Our local station is not briefed on the case," she said carefully. "This is a *Kidon* operation, and we're to have no contact with our locals."

If something went awry Israel could not afford to have her local representatives, not even Mossad representatives, involved even peripherally. *Kidon* operations always are compartmentalized and completely deniable.

"I understand," said Smetanin. "I think I can help. It will take the rest of the day to set it up. Where are you staying?"

"I haven't checked into a hotel yet. I'll look for someplace near-by."

"Why don't you stay here? It's safe, and there will be no record, not even in whatever alias you're using."

"That's very generous of you, Volodya. Thank you." There couldn't be a more secure, less conspicuous place in the city.

"It will be my pleasure, my dear. And I'm being entirely selfish. I don't often have such charming company, or any company at all, for that matter. Why don't you put your bag in the spare bedroom in back while I get to work on your request? There are snacks in the kitchen. I'll have to go out for a little while."

Nearly three hours passed before he returned.

He'd made the appropriate contacts, and after some shopping returned to Rue de Tournon carrying a string bag filled with components for the dinner he planned for them that evening. "It's set," he called on the way down the hallway to the kitchen. "We'll get all the manifests as soon as they're available. One of my people will deliver them here."

Sasha was relieved. "I don't know how to thank you, Volodya."

CHAPTER 9

Sasha's rendezvous with the Paris *Kidon* contact and Ronan was at a small café on *Avenue Wagrams*. She assured Volodya she would return in time for dinner and walked to the near-by Odeon Metro station, changed lines at *Les Halles*, and again at *Charles de Gaulle Etoile*, exiting at the next stop at *Place des Ternes*.

She knew the local contact, who used the alias Marc LeBrun for his cover in Paris as a travel writer. His real name was Moshe Leven. He was born in the coastal village of *Malgrat de Mar* in the sixties of parents who had survived the anti-Semitic persecutions of the likes of Klaus Barbie during the war. Finally tiring of the persistent, discreet anti-Semitism of the French, his parents immigrated to Israel when he was 12.

She found LeBrun at a table near the rear of the café, a carafe of house wine and three glasses on the table. With a smile of recognition, he stood when he saw her enter. He was a small, compact man with dark hair, a thin moustache, and an olive, Mediterranean complexion.

"Hi, Marc," she said, returning his embrace. "Good to see you again."

"Same here. Want to tell me what we're supposed

to be doing while we're waiting?"

When she finished he said, "So, kidnap if possible, assassinate if not, and capture whatever it is he's carrying. There's not much time to plan anything. What's the *memuneh* thinking?"

"He's using us, so he doesn't want any attribution if things go wrong, and we're the only ones available in Europe right now."

"I appreciate the *memuneh's* confidence, but I still don't like it. All we know is that the target will transit Paris on the way to Tehran. If he even leaves the airport he'll have company, and we'll have to wing it. The odds are against us."

"I can't argue with that. But we have our orders. We won't have much time to set up when he arrives."

"I have a car and weapons. I'll pass them out when Eitan arrives."

Fifteen minutes later, Ronan entered the café and took a seat next to Sasha. He was wearing a leather jacket and a baseball cap, and he looked like everyone's idea of a thug. The five o'clock shadow didn't help, either. He ordered a *demi*, a small glass of beer. When the waiter was gone, he asked, "Did our friend agree to help?" meaning Volodya Smetanin.

"Of course," she replied, "we'll know when the Russian is scheduled to arrive and which airport."

LeBrun was still dubious. "I still don't like it. There's a helluva lot of security at airports these days, including CCTV. Our best bet is if he leaves the airport, but why should he?"

He retrieved two wrapped packages from a leather satchel at his feet and placed them on the table. "Silenced Beretta Model 70's with two spare magazines each," he said.

"Assassins' weapons," rumbled Ronan. The Beretta fired especially nasty hollow point .22 rounds. "I need something with more punch just in case somebody shoots back. Get me a .45." He shoved his package with the Beretta back across the table at LeBrun.

"You're the boss, Eitan," said LeBrun. "But if we get into a gunfight, things are liable to go bad very fast."

"You're right, Moshe," said Ronan, using LeBrun's real name. "And I don't plan on things getting noisy. But if they do, I want to be ready. Now that I think about it, you might as well bring along an Uzi or two in the car."

LeBrun scowled and nodded. He was a careful man, which was why he was still alive, and this operation was too *ad hoc* to suit his sensibilities.

Sasha slipped her package into her bag. She was satisfied with the Beretta. It was the weapon she'd trained with for many months. "Thanks. Now we wait. I must get back to our friend. I'll call you as soon as I hear anything. Be ready."

Ronan nodded. "We'll rendezvous here as soon as we know."

The cold rain which had stopped when she left the *Rue de Tournon* had resumed with increased vigor, and she was glad to have borrowed an umbrella from Smetanin. The trip back to the apartment was uneventful, but the weight of the weapon in her bag was all the heavier for the uncertainty of success. She almost hoped it would turn out to be a wild goose chase.

Smetanin had been busy in the kitchen and by the time she returned and hung her dripping coat by the door, the table was laid with an excellent roast, potatoes, and asparagus with fresh bearnaise sauce. Her host opened a bottle of five-year-old *Chateauneuf du Pape* to complete the meal.

Later, over coffee, the perceptive Smetanin said, "You're worried, aren't you?"

"Yes. Frankly I don't give us much of a chance. I almost hope the target never appears or if he does, he never leaves the airport transit area."

"If their planning is perfect, it's likely you'll never see him," he agreed. "But you may have some luck. It's possible he could leave the airport. There may be no connecting flight until the day after he arrives."

"If he does leave the airport, it will likely be with an escort. And there are hotels at the airport itself. There is no reason I can imagine for them to leave Charles De Gaulle, at all. I don't think either the Russians or the Iranians would want him wandering around Paris carrying deadly anthrax spores in his pocket with or without guards."

"Are you sure you have enough people for this, Sasha. Why don't you let me organize some surveillance assistance for you?"

"You know we must restrict knowledge of the operation."

"I know, of course. But my people will ask no questions, and all they would do is surveil the target and fade away whenever you like. It would take a lot of the load off your shoulders, so you can concentrate on the harder things."

The old man was right. They would normally have a full team on such an operation, but there had been no time to set it up. Smetanin had local resources, and they must be reliable. She also knew Ronan would never permit it.

CHAPTER 10

Sasha waited nervously in the crowd for passengers to emerge from Passport Control and Customs in Charles De Gaulle International Airport's Terminal 2C. Two days had passed since the team's arrival in Paris, and Smetanin's contact had pinpointed the flight from Moscow that would bring Vinogradov to Paris.

Ronan and LeBrun were outside in a car waiting for her to report. She wore a transmitter/receiver under her coat, and an induction antenna hung around her neck that wirelessly transmitted sound to a tiny earbud. Her microphone was concealed in a sleeve.

She claimed a spot near the rope that separated the crowd from the swinging doors from which arriving passengers would spill after clearing Customs. People emerged a few at a time to head for the taxi queue outside the terminal or be greeted by someone waiting for them. A picture of Vinogradov was in her coat pocket, and she checked it surreptitiously trying to imprint the man's face on her mind.

According to the information board, the Moscow flight had arrived on time some forty-five minutes earlier. Passengers should have collected their luggage and passed through the formalities by now. She tried to read the tags on the luggage of those arriving as they came out the doors, and at last spotted a Moscow tag.

Vinogradov appeared at last wearing a heavy coat and hat. He carried only a small, carry-on bag.

"He's here," she murmured into the microphone.

Their fears that Vinogradov would never leave the airport transit area had been allayed when they saw his alias on the manifest for the evening flight from Moscow. The only flight to Tehran would not leave until the following morning.

She moved through the crowd toward the Russian but stopped when he was greeted by two men with Middle Eastern faces. One was heavy-set with a muscular build, and the other was thin with a dark ascetic face.

As anticipated, Vinogradov would have watchers in Paris.

She reported this to Ronan and LeBrun and followed the trio at a distance.

"They're heading for the Metro terminal," she said. She felt sudden hope that they were going into the city. The problem was that she would have to tail them alone. Ronan and LeBrun were in the car.

Vinogradov and his presumed Iranian minders boarded the CDGVAL Metro, a free intra-airport train, and she had no choice but to follow close behind doing her best to stay on their blind side. But the minders were vigilant and the brawny one's eyes raked over her as he scanned the other passengers.

After a short ride, they exited at the *Roissypôle* train station in Terminal 3. "They may take the RER train into town," she reported. She let them gain some distance on her before following.

But they did not take the train. Instead, they headed for doors that announced the entrance to the Novotel hotel. She followed across an open courtyard into the hotel in time to see the trio at the check-in counter. She reported this to Ronan.

The hotel was large, with a rear entrance linked to the terminal by the courtyard. The main entrance faced an airport road, and there was a parking lot for guests.

So, they planned to spend the night at the airport.

It took a while for Ronan and LeBrun to navigate the airport roads, but soon LeBrun joined her in the lobby. They headed for the bar and took seats.

"They've bedded down for the night," said LeBrun. He sighed, "I'll take the first watch here. Why don't you get a room and come down to spell me in a couple of hours?"

"OK, but I want to talk to Eitan first."

She found him in the car in the parking lot outside the main street entrance and slipped into the passenger seat. "LeBrun and I will take turns watching, but I don't like the set-up."

"Tell me about it."

"We can't do a take-down in the hotel lobby, and probably not inside the terminal. There would be too many witnesses, and the escape routes could be blocked. That leaves the open courtyard between the terminal and the hotel when they leave to put Vinogradov on the plane tomorrow morning, providing that is what they plan to do."

The scheduled departure for the plane to Tehran was seven in the morning which meant they would have to check in around five. It would still be dark, but the courtyard had lights. With luck there would be few people up and about at that hour, but they could not count on luck.

Ronan's forehead wrinkled in thought. "OK, I'll figure something out. We'll need to be ready by four a.m. Keep your coms open."

Ronan sat in the car for a long time thinking. Escape would be their main problem. Charles De Gaulle airport was huge, and the roadways within the airport proper were a confusing maze with a lot of dead-ends. They would need time to get away. He had the night to figure things out.

If he had a choice, he would abort the entire operation, but he did not have a choice. The *memuneh* had made it clear – Vinogradov and his toxic baggage could not be permitted to reach Tehran.

CHAPTER 11

A thick blanket of mist lay over the countryside surrounding Charles De Gaulle airport, and a light winter rain resumed as they set up the operation. By four a.m. Sasha had checked out of her room and taken up position in the lobby coffee bar which had only a handful of patrons at this pre-dawn hour. LeBrun waited inside the terminal across the courtyard with Ronan. None of them had slept.

She reached inside her handbag and felt the reassuring grip of the Beretta. She would use it that morning for the first time in a real operation, and she steeled her mind against self-doubt and the normal human abhorrence of taking another's life. Her targets were enemies in a deadly serious war, and sympathy for an enemy was unwise. She would rely on her training, which had been extensive and harrowing.

Again, she was in disguise – a dark, shapeless coat and a hat pulled down to conceal her blond hair. The black, horn-rimmed glasses were the final touch. She was chosen to remain in the hotel and follow the targets out the door because a woman, especially a non-descript woman, would be less likely to attract attention. Before leaving her room, she had wiped down every surface.

Ronan had devised a plan that gave them a thin chance of success, but speed in execution was essential if they were to get away. LeBrun had protested loudly that they should abort because chances of getting away were tenuous, at best.

Ronan quieted him with orders directly from the *memuneh.* Membership in *Kidon* meant that one did not question the *memuneh,* the man who interpreted God's will.

At 4:30 a.m. the elevators doors opened, and Vinogradov stepped out, one minder on each side. They paid their bill and headed for the exit to the courtyard and back to the terminal. As soon as they stepped outside, Sasha rose and hurried across the lobby to the exit, her hand on the pistol in her bag.

Through the glass doors, the courtyard looked empty in the pre-dawn gloom. The overhead lights cut dully through the mist and rain, and the trio ahead picked up their pace as they crossed the open space, anxious to get back inside. When they were half-way across the courtyard, Ronan and LeBrun emerged from the terminal and walked toward them. Sasha sped up until she was only ten feet behind.

The Iranian minders sensed danger. They were professionals who knew to trust their instincts. They both stepped in front of Vinogradov when they saw the two Israelies. They had not yet noticed Sasha behind them.

She was still drawing her Beretta when one of the Iranians raised a pistol and fired in the direction of Ronan and LeBrun. She saw LeBrun go down even as Ronan's .45 roared, and her Beretta spat silent death. Ronan fired twice, taking down the man who had shot

LeBrun, the heavy rounds from the .45 knocking him off his feet. Sasha's smaller round entered the other Iranian's skull and scrambled his brains. Vinogradov was left standing alone and confused.

LeBrun lay unmoving on the concrete several yards away. The gunfire had drawn the attention of the people inside the hotel, and white faces pressed against the windows.

"Get him to the car," shouted Ronan pointing at LeBrun. "I'll take care of the Russian. If I'm not there in a couple of minutes, get the hell out of here."

Sasha ran to LeBrun's still body. She prayed he wasn't dead. He groaned when she rolled him over, and she saw a bloodstained hole in his jacket on the right side of his chest. With luck, she thought, he'll survive, providing we all get away.

Straining under his weight, she helped LeBrun to his feet, and half-carried, half-dragged him to the thin line of trees that bordered the courtyard. On the other side of the trees was a drive with parking spaces where Ronan had pre-positioned a car. It wasn't the same car in which they had arrived. During the night, he'd found another and hot-wired it. Sasha managed to shove her nearly unconscious comrade into the back seat. She got behind the wheel, found the dangling ignition wires and started the engine. *Where was Eitan?*

Ronan shoved Vinogradov to the concrete and placed the barrel of his gun between the Russian's eyes. He had little time. Someone inside the hotel began to shout.

Ronan said to Vinogradov, "Where's the toxin concealed? Tell me now, or we'll find it on your body later." He pressed the .45 hard against the Russian's head.

Vinogradov was confused and frightened as he tried to process what was happening.

"The anthrax spores and whatever other poison you might be carrying," gritted Ronan. "Give them to me now and you might live."

Vinogradov finally understood. He fumbled in a pocket and produced a cigarette pack. "Everything's in there," he stammered.

There was little time to check the material. Ronan put the cigarette pack in his pocket as he shot Vinogradov. The Russian's head bounced on the concrete from the impact of the bullet. Ronan grabbed the Russian's bag, and ran for the tree line, hoping the car was still there.

He leapt into the passenger seat. "Drive out, turn right, and then take the first right. There's a drive there with parked cars. Pull into a slot so we're hidden from the road."

Sasha did as she was told. It was a narrow drive between tall office buildings, and there were several cars parked there that presumably belonged to airport personnel. She drove to the end and pulled into an empty space. Ronan lifted LeBrun from the back seat as though he weighed nothing and placed him in another car, the one in which they originally arrived. He got into the back seat with the wounded man and ordered Sasha to go." She had removed the hat and glasses, and her blond hair spilled over her shoulders.

It had been Ronan's decision that the Russian could not be permitted to live. Given the circumstances and the rushed nature of the operation, it was impractical to believe that even Mossad could abduct

Vinogradov and get him back to Tel Aviv. And even if they could, what would they have done with him then? The Russian's fate was decided even before they had begun.

It required fifteen minutes to navigate their way out of the airport and onto the A-1 back toward Paris. They spotted emergency response vehicles with flashing blue lights racing toward the airport on the other side of the multiple-lane A-1.

In the back seat, Ronan had removed LeBrun's jacket and shirt. There was a neat hole in the right side of his chest through which blood bubbled every time he took a ragged breath. Ronan placed his palm over the wound and pressed down. "We've got to get him to a doctor as soon as possible or he'll drown in his own blood," he said to Sasha. "Ask Tel-Aviv to find us one."

Sasha found the encrypted cell phone in her bag and punched a speed-dial number. The call was answered on the first ring. "Priority Alpha One," said Sasha – the code for a wounded operative in need of immediate assistance.

"I'm sending coordinates to your phone," was the response.

Within a few seconds, Sasha's phone buzzed, and she read a message which provided an address in the 17th Arrondisement. She handed Ronan the phone. He looked at the address and said, "That's good, the 17th is in the northern part of the city. Follow the signs for the A-1, get onto the *Périphérique Ouest*, and take the *Porte d'Asnières* exit. I'll direct you from there."

Their destination was near Montmartre in an upscale apartment building. A middle-aged man with an anxious expression stood at the curb and approached the car with some trepidation when they stopped. In a voice barely above a whisper, he said, "Are you visiting from the Mediterranean?"

The correct paroles exchanged, the man directed them to the building's underground garage, and he and Ronan carried LeBrun to an elevator that took them to a private apartment on the top floor.

"Let's get him on the table," said their host, leading them to a suite of rooms set up as a medical office with an examining room. They placed LeBrun on the examining table.

While he examined LeBrun, the man introduced himself as Doctor René Cassin. He was part of long-standing clandestine Mossad network of trusted physicians who lent their services to Israel whenever needed.

"Your friend is not in good condition," announced Cassin. "A chest wound is very serious, and the bullet is still in him. I'll have to operate. Can one of you assist?" He looked questioningly at Ronan and Sasha.

"I can help," said Ronan. "Tell me what to do."

"Good. Just hand me the instruments as I ask for them. Here, put these on." He handed a surgical mask and purple nitrile gloves to the big Israeli."

"Wait outside." Ronan waved Sasha toward the door.

She needed fresh air and decided to go outside. It was still dark, and few people were yet on the street. The morning's mist had dissipated, and the sky was at least temporarily clear, the stars visible. A short distance from the apartment she found a small, cobbled square with a restaurant on each corner and a stone staircase leading upward. She took the stairs and found herself in the heart of Montmartre. She'd never been here before, but she recognized the white domes of the *Sacre Cœur* church as it caught the first dim rays of the morning sun. She continued upward to the parapet overlooking the city and stood as the sun rose turning the Seine into a silver ribbon that bisected the city.

She lost track of time as the adrenalin drained from her body. She noticed with surprise that her hands were trembling, and she couldn't stop it. A kaleidoscope of images tumbled through her mind – the rushed travel to Paris, the desperation of their actions, a sleepless night at the airport hotel, and the shoot-out which resulted in Marc LeBrun's injury. But most of all it was the man she had killed, the small-caliber bullet entering his head just behind the left ear, the way life had fled his body in an instant and he'd crumpled to the ground. It had been her first *Kidon* assassination, and in a way, it angered her that it affected her so. Were Mossad officers permitted to have a conscience?

Poor LeBrun had doubted the plan and their ability to carry out a successful operation. He had been correct, and tragically so. LeBrun's wound was serious and could result in death. Sasha prayed that Doctor Cassin was good enough to save him.

The thought jolted her out of her reverie, and she hurried to return to the apartment where she found Ronan sunk deeply into a chair outside the operating theater, a Gauloise dangling from his lips. He looked up at her entrance and regarded her with tired eyes. "He'll live," he said. "It was close and thank God Cassin had a good store of blood for transfusion. LeBrun's lungs were filling, and he was down to a few liters by the time we got here."

"What do we do now?" Sasha was grateful her hands had stopped shaking. It was not something she would wish Ronan to see.

"Cassin will care for LeBrun while he heals. I think you should lie low at Volodya Smetanin's apartment for a while."

"How about you? What about the materials?"

"I don't think a plane or a train would be wise right now. I'll take LeBrun's car and drive south to Bellgarde then find a way across the border into Switzerland from there. I'll take the materials with me."

"Did you get everything?"

"I think so." He pulled a cardboard cigarette pack from his shirt pocket and pulled the silver wrapper with the cigarettes out. At the bottom of the pack were two tiny, sealed containers. "These apparently contain the spores. There are documents in the bag I grabbed, too."

Sasha shuddered at the sight of the deadly materials. "Will you leave immediately?"

"No. I'll spend the night here at Cassin's and make sure LeBrun is OK. You go to Volodya's. And forget the disguise. Your description is probably already being disseminated."

That was true, and she knew that Ronan was worried that his description was out there, as well. Given his size and build, he could not so easily disguise himself.

"Why don't you stay at Volodya's for a while, too?" she asked.

"No. We need to split up and go our separate ways. It's for the best, and it's standard procedure even after the most successful of operations."

"I know, but I'll still worry."

"I'll see you back in Vienna in a week or so. I'll be OK."

"I want to see Marc before I go."

Cassin had placed LeBrun in a guest bedroom where he rested in a large bed. Serum was still being transfused into him from a clear bag hanging on a rack beside the bed. The patient was still unconscious from the anesthetic, but he appeared to be resting comfortably. She squeezed his hand and silently wished him luck.

CHAPTER 12

Sasha found a worried Volodya Smetanin waiting at 13, Rue de Tournon. He enveloped her in surprisingly strong arms as soon as she stepped into the apartment. "My God," he exclaimed. "I was worried out of my head. You're all over the news."

It was just past noon, and clouds again had scudded in to darken the sky and drench Paris with freezing rain, keeping people off the streets. She'd taken a taxi from Cassin's apartment to the Etoile, where she'd switched to the Metro, emerging onto the street again on the Boulevard St. Germain. She was cold and wet by the time she arrived at Smetanin's.

"Things went south very fast," she said. "What are they saying on the news?"

"Oh, not much about the Russian, at least for the time being. The deaths of two Iranian Embassy officials in a shoot-out is the big story. They only reported that one of the assailants was wounded, and I had no idea which of you it was."

"It was LeBrun," she said. "One of the damned Iranians was faster than we expected. They were pros."

She assured him LeBrun was safe and well cared for, but she did not tell him anything about Cassin. Smetanin understood her caution, and she was grateful for his professional discretion.

"And my old friend Eitan? May I assume he's on his way out of town already? I could have had some of my people help."

"You know Eitan," she replied with more confidence than she felt. "He'll make his own way out. He suggested I might stay here with you for a few days."

"Of course, you're welcome." Smetanin regarded her for a moment longer from under shaggy brows and said, "You need to get out of those wet clothes and dry off. Take a hot bath. We'll have plenty of time to talk later."

The rain continued to drape Paris in shades of gray, leaving puddles and making the streets slippery. Through the tall windows of Smetanin's apartment Sasha watched Parisians scurry to cover, umbrellas providing the only splashes of color.

Smetanin was a warm, thoughtful host and evidently enjoyed the company of an attractive young woman, especially one from his native Russia. And she enjoyed his resonant voice as he spoke the sort of elegant Russian not heard since Tsarist times.

The days passed slowly, and she managed to coax him to share details of his long, colorful life. Volodya Smetanin's history was one that could only have been engendered by the upheaval of a world at war.

His father, a White Russian officer, sent his wife and infant son out of Russia when the Bolsheviks took over in Moscow. He remained behind with his comrades to fight the Reds. Several years later, after the fighting in Russia subsided, word reached his mother that his father had been killed in combat. Young Volodya's mother met and finally married a British ex-pat in Cairo, and they were drawn into the ex-pat community. The boy joined the Baden Powell movement, the Boy Scouts, and stayed with it, remaining active even as a young adult. One day in the late Thirties, Volodya's father appeared in Cairo, a ghost from the past, a man he had never known. His mother, now re-married faced the agonizing choice between her present husband and the scarred warrior who had returned from the dead. In the end, she chose her new husband, and Volodya's father disappeared, never to be heard from again, fading away like the Tsarist Russia he had defended.

Soon, the Second World War reached North Africa, and the British put up a stiff but seemingly hopeless resistance to Rommel's armored onslaught across the continent toward Suez. Volodya, joined the British forces where the survival skills honed by the Scouts were quickly employed. He was put to work as a front-line scout. He and his comrades had the job of creeping across no-man's land each night and slipping into the German lines to gather intelligence. A by-product of the task was the opportunity to slit the throats of German sentries. Thus, the dagger icon on Smetanin's wall which he dedicated to the memory of the men he had dispatched with it.

After the war, Volodya worked for a time for British Intelligence, but soon tired of the not-so-discreet prejudices of the British upper class who then populated MI-6. He moved to Paris and integrated himself into that city's burgeoning Russian ex-patriot community. Unfortunately, that community was rife with Soviet penetrations, as it had been since the days of the Comintern, and Volodya set about exposing and eliminating them. By the end of the Fifties, he had built a network of trusted confederates that stretched from Paris to Moscow. He had never known his father, but he detested the Bolsheviks for what they had done to his family and his country.

Sasha understood why Ronan trusted and revered this man so much. He was one of those who had experienced the convulsions of HISTORY writ large, one of many who put their lives on the line to resist a seemingly implacable foe. And he carried on the battle to this day. Sasha realized that it was an honor just to know such a man.

But Smetanin wore his past lightly. He delighted in telling old Soviet jokes and in preparing Russian delicacies for his guest.

"Tonight, we'll have some good Ukrainian borscht and *pelmeni*," he announced. "Then we'll finish up with caviar and vodka."

Despite his graciousness Sasha suffered from cabin fever and ennui. She had not ventured outside since returning to Rue de Tournon. A week had passed, and she judged the time had come for her to return to Vienna. Returning to Charles de Gaulle Airport would be personally harrowing, but she did not anticipate problems.

"I'm going to go out and find a travel agency," she said, "and reserve a seat on a flight to Vienna tomorrow. I'm afraid this will be our farewell meal."

For an instant, Smetanin's face betrayed disappointment at her announcement, but he recovered quickly. She thought he must be lonely here in his ancient apartment.

CHAPTER 13

Eitan Ronan wanted a cigarette badly. The blue pack of Gauloises in his jacket pocket was tantalizingly within reach. But the *memuneh* forbade smoking in his presence, and right now, the *memuneh* was staring at him from across his desk in Tel Aviv.

"I'm not so sure it was wise for you to carry Vinogradov's materials on your person," said David Shalev. "What if you'd been detained?"

Ronan shrugged. "I thought it was best. We had no contact with the embassy in Paris, you know."

"That could have been arranged easily enough. A courier could have been sent."

"I wasn't detained, and the materials are in our lab now. Why worry about what might have been? Sasha is back in Vienna, and Moshe is recovering. It was messy and public, but it was still a successful operation."

Shalev blinked at him. Ronan was one of his best operatives, but he tended to take risks Shalev would prefer to avoid. "I should have been there,' he mused, "you know, as protocol dictates." It was a long-standing tradition that the *memuneh* be in-country whenever a kidnapping or assassination was to be conducted.

"There wasn't time," growled Ronan, "and I don't

like that so-called protocol anyway. It's not so easy for the *memuneh* to travel these days as it was in the sixties."

Shalev shook his head. "Ah, well, Eitan, I won't argue with you. It seldom does any good. How did Sasha perform. This was her first job with *Kidon*, wasn't it?"

"She did fine. Some nerves, of course, but when it came time to act, she didn't hesitate. She took her target down."

"Good. The girl has promise, I think. Does she have a man somewhere, Vienna, perhaps?"

"Nothing permanent. She's not interested in permanent arrangements. She thinks it's impractical under present circumstances, so she keeps her distance. And she doesn't care for Austrians, anyway." Ronan was uncomfortable. He didn't like talking about Sasha; it was too much like informing on his own daughter.

"Eitan, we have a problem."

"A problem with Sasha?" Ronan was startled.

"No, of course not. I mean a problem with the Russians and Iranians. You managed to keep Vinogradov's materials out of the mullahs' hands, but there are many more scientists made desperate by the uncertainties in Russia today. I don't think the Russians have realized it yet, but they face an exodus of scientific and technical talent, and as in Vinogradov's case certain Russians are even facilitating it. Unfortunately, we can't intercept every one of them."

Ronan knew the *memuneh* was right. Soon Russian scientists with deadly skills would turn up in places like Syria and Iraq, as well as Iran. The threat to Israel would be cranked up several notches.

"The Iranians are the ones who concern us most," continued Shalev. "They have money and they have ambitions in the region. They chant 'death to Israel' as much as 'death to America,' and they mean it. Before too long, they'll be supplying Hezbollah with biological weapons."

"What can we do?"

"The Americans and others are becoming aware of the problem, and they can work with the Russian government now that Yeltsin's in charge. Some money will be found to try to keep the talent at home ..."

"But?"

"But the villains will keep trying, and many of the scientists will still be tempted."

"What can we do?" Ronan repeated.

"I'm thinking of going to the source."

"By which you mean ...."

"Thanks to your Russian walk-in and our own intelligence, we know who is running the show in Tehran. Perhaps we could find a way to slow them down, or at least send them a warning."

"Blue and White[9] in Tehran?"

"I know it's dangerous, but my thinking is tending in that direction. We still have some assets in Iran. Getting in and out is possible via Kurdistan in northern Iraq. The Americans and Brits are protecting the area now from Saddam Hussein, and they might be willing to give us some clandestine help. What do you think?"

"Only *Kidon* could do this."

Shalev nodded his agreement.

---

[9] "Blue and White" – Mossad.

"Shall I begin planning?"

"Take a look at the possibilities, methodologies, and the rest. Work up a plan of action and have it on my desk as soon as possible. I don't want to wait too long. I want the shock value of closely-spaced actions against them in Paris and Tehran. It won't stop them in the long run, but it will give them something to think about and make them more cautious."

Eitan Ronan's rough-hewn exterior concealed a sharp mind. Because he excelled at operational planning, David Shalev held him in high regard. Indeed, he was Shalev's favorite, a veteran of many battles with the wiles of a fox and the courage of a lion. These traits all would be required to conjure a workable scenario for an operation inside Iran. Shalev knew that the best he could hope for was less than a 50/50 chance of success.

MICHAEL

The Iranian helicopter turned to make another run at them and a series of eruptions threw snow high in the air as the machine gun rounds impacted in straight, parallel lines heading directly toward them. Michael held the girl tight, covering her body with his as he waited for the bullets to reach them.

CHAPTER 14

The muted beat of modern jazz drifted over the room, a murmur loud enough to be heard, but soft enough not to inhibit conversation. It was an upscale bar just off Geneva's Quai Wilson. In the rear, Michael Mossberg sat quietly in the semi-darkness and stared at the half-empty glass of Campari and soda on the opposite side of the table and the vacant chair behind it.

It was like a magic trick. When the glass was full, a beautiful girl sat opposite him; when it was half-empty, she had disappeared. The glass was a lingering relic of Mariana, who had vacated the chair some minutes earlier. It was all that was left of their brief affair. The girl had been hurt when he broke it off. But it couldn't be helped.

This was a recurring theme of Mossberg's existence. Long-term relationships were not advisable, especially with foreigners. "Long-term" for Michael could be a few days or a few years, or his life could be snuffed out in a few minutes. He led a dangerous life, and it would be unfair to bring an unwitting girl into it. But Michael was a man, and he had his needs. Still, it was unsatisfying and sad.

Buy Another Day

Mrs. Delacort, a spritely 71-year-old widow was in love with the handsome Spaniard who lived in the apartment across the hall. His slightly olive skin and piercing black eyes made for an irresistible combination. At her age, she harbored no romantic illusions, and the many young women she'd seen coming out of his door made romance a longshot in any event. But his French was exquisite, and he was unfailingly polite and had even looked after her cat when she travelled to visit her daughter in Zürich. He travelled frequently because of his work as a travel agent, and she missed him during these absences.

Mossberg was tall and lanky with unruly black hair which he wore stylishly long. He dressed well and was a devotee of French Armagnac. His fluency in foreign languages had attracted the attention of Mossad when he was still at university. Now at the age of thirty-two he had made seven languages his own. While serving in the IDF, he distinguished himself in Southern Lebanon against Hezbollah. He did not resist Mossad's recruitment pitch.

His current assignment had taken him to Switzerland under Spanish cover with the task of unravelling the secrets of the bank accounts controlled by Russian oligarchs, particularly the empire of a Russian criminal who resided in Zürich.

Mossberg was not his real name, although it was the name by which most people knew him. The name his parents had given him was Menashe Ben Ari. The Mossad had christened him with a new identity because it better concealed his origins. Mossberg was the son of Iranian immigrants who had moved to Israel in the

1950's as part of Operation Cyrus.[10] The Iranian community in Israel strove to retain its cultural identity, and Mossberg had grown up in a Farsi-speaking home, a fact which made him of particular value to the Mossad. After two years of specialized training in the Negev, he now had been a *Kidon* team member for three years.

All of this made him the ideal candidate for the operation planned by Eitan Ronan.

Kidon team members seldom visit Mossad Headquarters. Contact is normally carried out in clandestine meetings at remote sites. Thus, Michael Mossberg was curious and hopeful about the call to meet Ronan in Geneva and hoped it meant action and a way to distance himself from the guilt he was now feeling about Mariana.

His work in Switzerland, while important, did not assuage his desire to bring more direct measures to bear on Israel's enemies.

Ronan had chosen the Noga Hilton hotel on the Quai du Mont Blanc for the meeting. It was an ostentatious choice, perhaps, but the larger and pricier the hotel, the greater the anonymity and privacy afforded to well-heeled guests.

Mossberg hadn't seen the leader of his team for several months. They embraced when Ronan let him into the room. "You're looking well, Eitan." He glanced around the grandly appointed room. "The *memuneh* must really like you to foot the bill for this party. What's in the minibar?"

---

[10] Operation Cyrus: In 1952 some 30,000 Iranian Jews immigrated to Israel under the auspices of this program.

Ronan smiled, something that could be menacing to those who didn't know him, like a grizzly bear showing his teeth. "The minibar is off-limits, I'm afraid. David will only go so far. But I just brewed a pot of fresh coffee."

Mossberg sighed with disappointment. In his view luxurious surroundings merit luxurious behavior.

Ronan poured coffee into two porcelain cups emblazoned with the Hilton emblem and handed one to Mossberg. The two made an interesting contrast: Mossberg a debonair Mediterranean version of Cary Grant and Ronan, a rock of a man with a rough exterior. But underneath it all, they were the same.

Ronan took a seat and invited Mossberg to follow suit. "We have job for you, Michael. How would you feel about representing the Blue and White in Iran?"

Mossberg's eyes widened slightly. He'd never been to his parents' homeland, and he was intrigued. "I like it. What's the mission?"

"There is an annoying person we'd like to eliminate."

"Tell me more. Who else is on the team?"

Ronan sipped the hot coffee and lit a Gauloise before answering. "Just you, Michael. You'll be working with the MEK[11] on the inside." His eyes never left Mossberg as he judged the man's reaction.

"Do we really trust them? They must be penetrated. Iranian Intelligence is pretty damned good, and they've killed a hell of a lot of *Mojahedin* members." This was unusual, *Kidon* usually worked in closely knit,

---

[11] People's Mojahedin Organization of Iran or the Mojahedin-e Khalq.

well-coordinated teams.

It was a good question and one Ronan had anticipated. "We're not following normal operational protocol on this one, Michael. There is a timing factor and arranging for an entire team to infiltrate Iran would take more time than the *memuneh* has given us. We still have some assets there, especially in Tehran. We even have some safehouses that were established before 1979, and we are in contact with some carefully vetted people there. These are the ones who will be working with you."

"What's the in and out?"

"We'll have you fly in commercially as a Spanish businessman. You might be able to leave the same way, but you'll have the option of a clandestine exfiltration with the MEK's help."

"Across the border into Kurdistan, I assume?"

Ronan nodded, appreciating the quickness of Mossberg's mind. "The Kurds aren't very pleased with the Mullahs since Khomeini put down their rebellion and murdered their leader, Abdul Rahman Ghassemlou, in Vienna a couple of years ago. We can count on their help if we need it."

"What intelligence do we have on the target?"

"Mehdi Asadi is the head of Iran's biological weapons development program, and he's been recruiting Russian scientists, taking advantage of the current mess in the wake of the dissolution of the Soviet Union. Of course, the KGB has been helping Iranian intelligence for years now."

"And you think killing one man will stop them?"

"No, but the *memuneh* thinks it'll slow them down and give them something to think about. They've already set up a bio-weapons program in Marzanabad. If you're successful, we'll see about a bigger strike there in the future."

"So, I'm a guinea pig?" He was actually thinking sacrificial lamb.

"Somewhat more than that, Michael, but I can't minimize the danger. But you'll have help. The MEK has been collecting intelligence on Asadi which they'll share with you in Tehran."

CHAPTER 15

Mossberg liked Madrid, a city of much charm, amazing history, and bodaciously beautiful women. His alias Spanish passport ensured smooth passage through the arrivals controls at Barajas International Airport, and an expensive taxi ride dropped him at the doors of a discreet hotel near the Alcala Gate.

He'd chosen a morning flight to allow himself a day to savor the city's charms and make certain his Spanish language skills remained sharp. So, he spent the day wandering up and down the Serrano, amused as always by the architectural eyesore of the American Embassy at the top of the street. The ugly 1960's style building was a monument to the Americans' lack of taste. He had mixed feelings about the Americans. They were like spoiled rich kids with too many toys.

The annual deluge of tourists would not descend on Spain for a few months, so the streets, shiny from a winter rain, were not clogged. *Madrileños* hurried along the broad sidewalks in winter coats bringing little business to the high-end shops along the Serrano. Mossberg longed for the Mediterranean sun of southern Spain, Andalusia, which reminded him so much of Israel.

That evening he enjoyed a quintessentially

Spanish meal of roast lamb and green salad at Cristobal's, a small restaurant in the north of the city he'd discovered on a previous visit and washed it down with a robust house Rioja from a pitcher. Not for the first time he agreed that Spanish pride in their cuisine was justified.

The next morning, he visited the Embassy of Iran on Calle de Jerez in a relatively affluent neighborhood in the Nueva España district of Madrid. The visa process was surprisingly uncomplicated, and within an hour Michael was back on the street.

Two days later he debarked from an Austrian Airlines flight onto the tarmac of Mehrabad International Airport and for the first time in his life breathed Persian air. He had, of course, been born in Israel, but like most Israelis of Iranian origin, his parents were proud of their Iranian identity. Their ancestors had been in Persia since the time of Nebuchadnezzar, and the cultural roots ran very deep. Even now, forty years after their immigration, they still spoke Farsi at home, and it was the first language Michael had learned. So, he had grown up speaking Farsi and eating Iranian food

Mehrabad, Tehran's international airport, was old. It had begun service in 1938 and been modernized and expanded over the years and now included an Air Force base. It was conveniently located in the southwestern quadrant of Tehran.

Despite the nature of his mission, Michael was

excited to be in the city of his parents' birth. The sky was overcast, but it was not particularly cold on this February day. After a short walk to the terminal he passed through a perfunctory passport control, collected his single checked bag and caught a cab at the curb outside the terminal.

The cab was a Mercedes several years old but kept meticulously clean. The driver was an older man with his grizzled gray hair closely cropped. He wore thick glasses with plastic frames and a padded jacket. Michael gave him the name and address of the hotel in District 2 where he had reserved a room and settled back to enjoy the ride into town. The air here was somehow different, as though it were laden with exotic, yet familiar spices. Michael knew it was only in his imagination, a tenuous shadow of home and his parents.

As they approached a huge plaza just outside the airport he immediately recognized the white marble inverted "y" of the Azadi Tower which commemorated over 2,500 years of Imperial Iran. Originally named *Shahyad* for the Shah who built it, the tower had been renamed after the 1979 revolution. *Azadi* means "freedom" in Farsi, an irony given the dark restrictive nature of the theocracy which now ruled the country. Still, it was a handsome construction in Michael's eyes.

District 2 where his hotel was located is in the northernmost section of Tehran, and the route there took him through the very heart of the city. Michael was surprised at the broad avenues and modern buildings. Had he not known better, this could be a modern city in any Western European country. The streets were filled with automobiles and trucks with a liberal sprinkling of motorbikes and scooters.

He paid particular attention to the motorbikes.

But this was not Western Europe. The women he saw all wore *hijabs* or *rousari* of different colors that covered most of their hair. There were no burkas, but he knew women were required to wear a *chador* in and around mosques. It seemed there were not many women on the streets. In many areas he saw groups of tough-looking youths who cast suspicious glances in all directions. Some of the boys carried clubs.

"Who are those guys?" he asked the driver.

"Those punks?" The driver jerked his head in the direction of one of the groups. "They're *basij*, mostly ignorant country boys brought into the capital to help keep order."

"How do they do they do that?"

"Any way they wish. You must be careful of them. If you see them coming, get out of the way. Don't look them in the eye. They'll beat you, or worse, and enjoy doing it."

Michael studied the young toughs and entered them in his calculations. The driver was talkative, and his speech surprisingly cultured.

"How long has this been going on?" asked Michael.

"For some weeks now, since the troubles. Ever since Imam Khomeini died there has been a struggle between those who wish to liberalize society and the conservatives who favor a stricter regime. When Rafsanjani was elected, we had some hope. He wanted reform, and the people supported him, but things got out of hand. There were demonstrations, and the hardliners reacted. They feared the revolution was failing."

"So, they're still cracking down?"

"It's been worse than ever lately. Many people have ended up in prison."

"Forgive me," said Michael, "but you speak very freely. Is that wise, given the circumstances?"

The driver hunched over the steering wheel and shrugged. "What difference does it make?"

Curious, Michael asked, "What do you mean?"

The driver hunched his shoulders even more as though he expected a blow and replied in a weary voice, "I was once a university professor. I taught history. I had a family and a nice house. Now I have only this automobile and I live in a hovel of an apartment. I've seen the inside of the Ayatollah's prison and managed to come out alive, unlike my son and daughter."

Michael's voice was gentle. "What happened?"

"This was in the eighties while Khomeini was still consolidating his power. My children were still young, only fifteen and seventeen. They took part in a few demonstrations and were accused of being members of the People's *Mojahedin*, a group that opposed the Islamic State. They weren't, of course. They were simply young and foolish. But it made no difference. They were lined up with others against a prison wall and shot. Then they released me. My wife soon died of grief."

"I'm sorry." There was nothing more he could say.

The driver lapsed into moody silence.

After nearly an hour they arrived at the hotel. Michael handed the driver three times the fare. "May God bless you, sir."

"Thank you, but God has cursed me and this

country."

Michael lugged his bag into the hotel. The lobby was small, with a few chairs and a reception desk behind which sat a man of indeterminate age and an air of disinterest.

Michael's cover was as a Spanish businessman named Alfredo Morales in Iran to purchase carpets. He signed the hotel register and showed his Spanish passport. He spoke in purposely accented English.

"You'll have to leave the passport with me," said the receptionist."

"I don't think so."

"It's the rule." He held out his hand.

"I'm not giving you my passport. I'll be needing it. Tomorrow I travel to Isfahan."

"Then I'll hold the passport until then." The receptionist still held out his hand, palm up, waggling his fingers impatiently.

"No, but maybe you can hold this instead." Michael placed a small stack of rials in the receptionist's hand.

The receptionist looked at the money, calculated the amount, and quickly stuffed the bills in his pocket. "Maybe we can forget the rules this one time." He handed over a room key and turned away.

Michael took the creaky elevator to the third floor and found his room. There were a sink and a shower, but the toilet was down the hall. It was sparse, but clean, and the heating worked. The mattress was of dubious comfort. He opened his bag and spread some brochures advertising an imaginary carpet store in Madrid across the bed for the benefit of anyone who might be interested in searching the room.

He checked his watch. It was still early afternoon which left several hours before he was to make the first rendezvous with the team which was to assist him. It was not a "team" in the usual Mossad sense, and this still worried him. The people he would meet were locals, Iranians, and it would be tricky because there was no reason to trust them other than Eitan Ronan's assurances. Michael had no idea how Ronan had made this determination or how trustworthy the MEK might be.

First contact was to take place later in the afternoon with an alternate the following day. The venue was a small cafe near a park about a mile from the hotel. This was too close to his hotel for Michael's taste, but he had not devised the plan. Intelligence officers are often dependent on the planning of others. At any rate, if all went well, he would not be in the hotel the next day.

Michael changed into a pair of khaki slacks and a white shirt and pulled a blue, padded jacket from his bag. This was the sort of outfit that would not look out of place on a Tehran street. He left the hotel and began to walk. Not having the luxury of casing the city beforehand other than basic familiarization with a map, he had to improvise a surveillance detection route. After two hours of rambling, stepping in and out of shops, reversing his route, and once or twice ducking out of sight and waiting to see what happened, he was satisfied he had no tail.

But that did not mean he would not be stepping into a trap at the rendezvous. All the precautions in the world would be of no use if the meeting itself was a trap.

A clandestine meeting with a stranger is always

a delicate matter. A lot can go wrong. In this case, even if Eitan Ronan vouched for the contact, a lot could have happened to change the equation. The authorities may have identified the contact as a hostile and coerced him under their control. Or they could simply substitute their own asset in the contact's place.

Michael had a description of the person he was to meet – a young man in his mid to late twenties with black hair, a light beard, and brown eyes – a description that could apply to the majority of young Iranian men. But the contact had a scar on the left side of his face, and the lobe of his left ear was missing.

He made his way to the meeting site and took a seat in the park across the street. There were not many people about at this time of day. After fifteen minutes, he got up and circled the block, alert for hostile indicators. Again, he saw nothing that aroused his suspicion.

He returned to the park and waited. Five minutes before the appointed time he saw a man who fit the contact's description enter the coffee shop. He was too far away to confirm the facial features, but the age was right. The man was slender, about five feet ten inches tall and dressed casually. His gate was slow and his manner slightly furtive, which simultaneously amused and worried Michael. This guy was no pro. With a last glance over his shoulder, the man entered the coffee shop.

Michael scanned the area once more before crossing the park and entering the shop. There were only a few customers seated at small, round tables drinking fruit juices and tea. He spotted the contact at a table in the rear. So far, so good. He wasn't getting any hostile vibes, although that would mean nothing if an ambush were well planned and executed. Michael wished he had a weapon, even a knife, but he did not.

He walked toward the contact's table with a broad grin. "Fareed!" he said. "I haven't seen you since university. How is our friend Arash?"

The contact, whose name was not Fareed and who was much too young to have attended university with Michael, stood and said, "Arash has moved to Isfahan."

The proper sign and counter-sign exchanged, the two embraced and kissed one another's cheek as is the Iranian custom among friends.

They ordered fruit juice from the proprietor. When they were alone, the contact said in a quiet voice, "Your Farsi is excellent."

"It should be," said Michael, "It's my native language."

"You're Iranian?" The contact was surprised and a little frightened.

Michael placed a hand on his arm across the table. "Don't be alarmed. My parents are from Tehran, but I wasn't born here."

"Oh." The contact was embarrassed. "I didn't know what to expect. I thought we might be speaking English."

"That would not have been wise. Now, what is the plan?"

"You will leave the hotel tomorrow and come with me. We have the safehouse prepared."

"Excellent."

"I'll pick you up at the hotel early tomorrow."

"Good."

"By the way, my name is Farhood."

"Ah, *the lion cub*," said Michael, recognizing the meaning of Farhood's first name. "Good name. Pleased to meet you."

Farhood grinned, his nervousness dissolving. He looked expectantly at Michael.

"My name is Barid," said Michael.

"*The messenger.* That's appropriate," grinned Farhood.

They ordered a light meal and ate in silence. The place was not appropriate for operational talk. After a half-hour, they left, the plans for the next day set.

Michael returned to the hotel and took a hot shower. With nothing to do he lay on the bed and watched Iranian television until he fell asleep. Things would begin in earnest tomorrow, and he would need all his strength and energy until he could get out of this country.

If he could get out.

CHAPTER 16

Farhood picked him up in an old Toyota sedan. The desk clerk wished him a safe journey to Isfahan as he carried his bag out the door. Michael almost wished he actually were going to Isfahan to buy carpets.

After a block, Michael asked Farhood to pull over and switch places. He wanted to check for surveillance and did not trust the younger man's talents.

They drove for an hour and a half around town, then headed north toward *Pas de Qaleh*, a scenic route through the mountains. Michael saw nothing alarming.

"OK," he said to Farhood. "Where do we go?"

Farhood directed him to an apartment building in a quiet neighborhood in District 8 just south of West Golbarg Street. This was the southeastern section of Tehran. The building was one of several built around a small green park.

As they entered the building Farhood explained, "This was my uncle's apartment."

The elevator was not working, so they took the stairs to the fourth floor where Farhood unlocked the apartment door.

They were greeted by a young woman standing in the middle of the room pointing a pistol at them. She lowered it immediately when she saw Farhood, who laughed out loud. Turning to Michael, he said, "Barid, this is my sister Seriyah. As you can see, she is very security conscious."

The girl embraced her brother. "I was so worried. You were away longer than expected."

"Our new friend here insisted on driving around in circles for a long time," said Farhood.

Michael was not amused. Having a weapon pointed at him was no laughing matter, regardless of who was pointing it. In this case the "who" was a slight, raven-haired beauty wearing jeans and a white wool turtleneck. The pistol, which Michael recognized as a Glock 17, looked big in her hands, but she had not trembled or displayed fear when aiming it at them. She now stood unsmiling, regarding him with a measuring eye. Despite his annoyance, the Lothario in Michael was stirred by the sight of this fierce young woman.

"Um, Seriyah, could you please make us some coffee, and then we'll talk," said Farhood.

With a final curious glance over her shoulder at Michael she headed for the kitchen as Michael admired her retreating form.

The apartment was not large, but it was well appointed with overstuffed furniture, a rich carpet covering the parqueted floor, and several impressive Muslim artworks adorning the walls.

"You said this was your uncle's apartment?" asked Michael.

"Yes. Let's go into the kitchen and help Seriyah. We can talk in there."

They sat on wooden chairs around the table as Seriyah poured thick, dark coffee into small cups. Farhood explained that their uncle had been a doctor at

Milad Hospital. He was a bachelor, and when he died five years ago, he had left the apartment to Farhood and Seriyah, his closest relatives. Their family name was Esfahani. The siblings, who had lost their parents, now lived in the apartment. They operated a small family grocery not far away.

Michael was curious. These two young people could not possibly have been Mossad safehouse keepers before 1979. They had been mere children at the time. "How is it you came to be involved with us?" he asked.

"Our uncle confessed to us on his deathbed that he had cooperated with Israel for years. He was a very free-thinking, democratic man. We were both surprised and delighted at the prospect of taking over for him."

"It could not have been an easy decision. It carried a lot of danger for you."

Farhood and Seriyah looked at one another. "No," said Seriyah in a quiet voice. "The decision was not hard, at all. In fact, we welcomed it."

"You don't approve of the regime?"

Seriyah's dark eyes lit with anger. "We hate the regime and all it stands for. They have dragged our country back into the Dark Ages."

Farhood placed an arm around his sister's shoulders. "You see, Barid, we are lucky to be alive. Several years ago, before my uncle's death, we were both imprisoned, suspected of being members of the *Mojahedin*. We were both students, and we were caught up in a demonstration. The security service rounded everyone up and threw us into Evin Prison. We were there for several weeks and ... suffered severe hardships." He touched his mutilated ear. "Most of our friends were murdered in the prison, and we were fortunate that our uncle still had enough influence to arrange for our release. But we had seen the dark underbelly of the regime up close. We are happy to help you in any way we can if it hurts them."

Michael recalled the taxi driver's story and shuddered inwardly at the horrors these two must have experienced. "I'm very sorry," he said. "I can't imagine what you must have gone through."

"No," said Seriyah with downcast eyes. "And you don't want even to imagine it."

"So, you see," interjected Farhood, "we are very motivated."

But Michael saw a problem – a very serious problem. "I can appreciate your feelings," he said, "but you've had no training. This is a very dangerous operation."

"Tell us what you want us to do, and we'll do it, anything," said Seriyah. "We don't care about the danger."

Not for the first time, Michael silently cursed Eitan Ronan. Was this really the best the Mossad could do in Iran? True, the networks had been down for well over a decade leaving little more than basic support capabilities, but he had expected more than having to work with simple safehouse keepers, little more than well-meaning children, at that. The *memuneh* must be out of his mind to have sanctioned this.

He said, "I appreciate your enthusiasm, but enthusiasm is no substitute for experience."

"Just tell us what you want us to do," repeated Seriyah, defiance now coloring her voice.

Michael sighed, the idea of aborting the mission and slipping quietly back to Spain broke the surface of his thoughts like a breaching whale, but he quickly repressed it. He was here in Tehran. The least he could do would be to check every possibility.

Mossad's remaining apparatus in Iran was supported by the MEK and the National Council of Resistance in Iran. They were now allied with the Kurdistan Workers Party, the PKK, via its Iranian offshoot, the Democratic Party of Iranian Kurdistan, the PDKI, which had been fighting Tehran since 1979. These were organizations with their own agendas, and the MEK even had cooperated with Saddam Hussein for a time. But they now served the Mossad as allies of convenience. It was a delicate, dangerous business. The PDKI operated out of the newly established Kurdistan across the border into Iran, and they were hardened fighters.

"You said you were jailed for being members of the *Mojahedin*. Were you?" asked Michael.

Farhood gave him a crooked smile. "No, we weren't then. But obviously we are now."

"How were you briefed on my arrival and mission?"

"A brother who received the orders from the PKK. It was all rather sudden."

"Can we expect assistance from these brothers?"

Farhood frowned. "I suppose so, but we weren't briefed on that."

"But you have means of contact?"

"Of course."

"But you're not cutting us out of the operation!" Seriyah's voice was harsh, and she pounded a small fist on the table."

"I agree," said Farhood, and there was

belligerence in his eyes, too. "We've waited too long to strike back, and if you're thinking of trying something without us, you can just go to the airport and fly back to wherever you came from."

Just what I was thinking. Michael knew, in fact, that without these two, he was blind, deaf, and dumb in Tehran. He said nothing for a few beats, then, "Calm down. That's not what I was thinking. Not to be too much of a downer, but it's more than just possible we'll need an escape route."

Farhood was puzzled. "But I thought you would leave the same way you came – just fly out of the country."

Michael smiled at the naïveté. "Farhood, I'm afraid it's a fact that intelligence operations seldom go exactly as planned. You and Seriyah must consider the possibility that you won't be able to continue your lives here if something goes wrong. You might have to leave the country, too. And none of this can occur without careful planning and some solid assistance."

The brother and sister were shocked. Clearly, they had never considered the idea that they could not remain in Iran.

Michael decided to let the idea gestate for a while. It was still quite possible the two would abandon the operation. "First things first," he said. "Seriyah had a gun. If my briefing was correct, there should be a cache of weapons in this apartment, along with other equipment."

"There is," said Farhood, his enthusiasm returning. "Let me show you."

Michael followed him to a back bedroom where Farhood showed him how to open the false back of a closet. Inside, in a neatly arranged row, were five Glock 17s. There was a missing slot where Serivah's pistol had been stored. There were fifty boxes of 9mm ammunition and extra magazines for the Glocks. In addition, there were maps, escape and evasion packages, walkie-talkies, what looked like 20,000 American dollars in neat stacks, and ten hand grenades. All this stuff was over ten years old, but Michael was confident of the Glocks and ammo. The money could come in handy. Forget the walkie-talkies – after so much time the electronics would be unreliable, and the decade old batteries would be depleted and incapable of holding a charge.

Apart from the equipment he expected there was a sealed package. Turning to Farhood, Michael asked, "Is this what your contact left with you?"

"Yes," replied Farhood. "He said to treat it carefully and not to open it."

The package had not been tampered with, and for this Michael was grateful. Farhood and his sister could follow orders. Maybe there was still hope.

Michael checked one of the Glocks. It was clean and in good operating order.

With evident pride Farhood said, "We've maintained all the equipment in working order. I break down the guns and clean them once a month. Of course, we haven't dared carry a weapon on the street, especially during the recent troubles. It would be a death sentence if caught."

"You've done well, Farhood, very well, indeed."

Michael loaded two 17-round mags and slid one into a pistol. The other he put in his pocket. He noted with approval that the ammunition was hollow point.

The nine-millimeter might not have the knock-down power of a .45, but with the right ammo, it would do the job. Dangerous or not, he would not be unarmed from now until he escaped Iran.

"Let's go back to the kitchen and have some more coffee, if you don't mind," he said. "We need to discuss some things."

Once they were again seated around the table with cups recharged, Michael asked, "You know the identity of the target?"

This time it was Seriyah who replied. "Of course. You mean Mehdi Asadi, and we've been investigating him."

"Investigating him ...?"

"Watching him."

This was alarming. Despite their enthusiasm, or maybe because of it, these two amateurs might well have taken risks and exposed themselves."

Seriyah sensed his concern. "How else do you think the information you require could be collected? You need not worry. No one saw us."

Michael hoped she was right. "Does Asadi have security?"

"There is a guard at his home, and he has a driver we assume to be armed. But he never varies his routine, and they seem complacent. They feel safe here in Tehran."

That made sense. "Tell me how you did it."

"Over the past month, ever since we received instructions, we've worked to determine his routine, when he leaves home, when he returns, his route to work. We did this in stages. First, we observed his house, and this was probably the most dangerous step as a lot of high government officials live in his neighborhood. So, we watched his street only a few times and never on consecutive days to determine when he left and the direction he took. Then we staged along his route, which was less dangerous. We knew where he worked, so it was not difficult. What we found is that he follows the same route every day at the same time."

This was encouraging. Maybe he'd misjudged these youngsters. "Did you get the motorbike?" he asked.

"Yes," said Farhood. "We used some of the money from the cache."

"Good. You have it near-by?"

"We have a storage room in the basement of this building. It's down there."

"It's in good operating order?"

"It is."

Mehdi Asadi lived in a villa in the *Shahrak-e Gharb* neighborhood in northern Tehran, the most affluent part of the city. The villa had been expropriated from a former official of the Shah's government. It was surrounded by a high, iron fence with a presumably armed security guard stationed at the entrance. Asadi was picked up each morning at seven a.m. by a driver in a government Mercedes. His route to work was not encouraging. At attack near his residence was unwise, given the other high government officials in the neighborhood, all with guards. But his route to work was mostly over large, high-speed highways. Near his house, he entered the Hemat Highway and drove only a short distance before turning north onto the Chamran Highway, and a few moments later onto Molla Sadra Street. It was at this point that they would begin to look for a suitable ambush site. Asadi worked in a building dedicated to the Presidential Deputy for Science and Technology on Ladan Street, a few blocks north of Molla Sadra."

"Do you think his car is armored?" asked Michael.

Farhood frowned. "I'm not sure."

"Have you ever seen the driver or Asadi roll down a window?"

"Yes. The driver does this when he waits for Asadi. He's usually smoking a cigarette."

"That's good," said Michael. "It means the car is not armored."

CHAPTER 17

Mehdi Asadi's villa was a large, ornate affair covered with white stucco. It was surrounded by a high, wrought iron fence with electronically operated gates.

Michael had Farhood drive him through the neighborhood so he could confirm their assessment of the area and Asadi's route to work. They were correct. Most of the route was via busy freeways with limited exits. To be successful, the operation required an escape route, and that meant it would have to be mounted toward the end of Asadi's commute, near his place of work. Even this was not ideal. It was largely a business area with broad streets and none of the small, dark alleys that might offer good opportunities for escape and evasion, places where they could disappear easily. Michael estimated they would be at the limit of operational security.

The call was his, and he knew Ronan would support whatever decision he made. Unlike a normal operation, Michael had no way to communicate with Tel Aviv other than literally word of mouth via a string of intermediaries he did not know: the *Mojahedin*, the PKK, etc. That would take more time than he had. He was loath to have come this far and do nothing. But he needed more assets than just this boy and girl. Getting away after the operation was likely to be more dangerous and complicated than the operation itself.

Karzan Bashur preferred his native mountains to Tehran. He did not like descending into the world of the Persians. As an ethnic Kurd and member of the PKK he was based in the newly established Kurdistan in northern Iraq, across the Northwestern frontier of Iran. He could speak fluent Farsi, but the language felt like excrement in his mouth. Still, he would work with the *Mojahedin* so long as they opposed the corrupt regime of the Mullahs.

Three days earlier he had made the hazardous journey across snow-covered mountains into Iran and made his way to a small Kurdish village south of Marivan near the border, where he'd met a contact who had hidden him in the rear of a truck among packing crates for the long, nine-hour drive to Tehran. The capital city was especially dangerous these days, he knew, with roving bands of *Basij* and a heavier than usual presence of security forces due to recent political unrest.

He was out of sorts and cautious about meeting an Israeli spy. He waited at a PDKI safehouse in one of the poorest sections of southern Tehran, an area where it was dangerous to be on the street. As soon as the meeting was over he would make the journey back into the mountains.

At the appointed hour there was a knock at the door – two long, one short. A young Iranian man entered followed by an older, taller man with tousled black hair and black eyes who also looked Iranian. Karzan was immediately on-guard. *Where was the Israeli?*

But he recognized the younger man as the same person to whom he'd transmitted the orders and a package several weeks earlier, a *Mojahedin* member named Farhood. "What is this?" he asked.

Mojahedin members were always being caught by the Iranian security service, and meeting with them on enemy territory was never routine. For this reason, he had taken precautions.

"*Baradar*[12]," said Farhood, "this is Barid, the man we were waiting for. It is important that we talk with you, and we are grateful you came."

Karzan gestured at a rickety table in one corner of the room, away from the window. He noted that the tall man identified only as Barid took the chair in the corner facing the rest of the room.

"We may need the assistance of your organization to get out of Iran following the operation," said Michael. Under the table he kept his hand on the grip of the Glock in his belt under his jacket.

Karzan eyed him suspiciously, taking careful note of the hand under the table. "That was not part of the request we received. Our role was simply to arrange for the arrival and reception of an Israeli agent in Tehran and to deliver a package. And you do not look like an Israeli. You're going to have to tell me more." Karzan did not like the idea of sticking around longer than necessary.

A bulky man with a heavy tangle of beard and a

---

[12] *Baradar* – Farsi for "brother."

shaved head appeared from a doorway Michael assumed led to a bedroom. The man carried a Kalashnikov and positioned himself so he could cover both Michael and Farhood.

This was not entirely unexpected. In Karzan's place, Michael would have brought back-up to meet an unknown foreign agent in hostile territory, too. But unsurprising as it was, it was still unwelcome. He looked inquiringly at Karzan who exhibited a particularly nasty grin.

"Please, place both of your hands on the table," ordered the Kurd.

Reluctantly, Michael released his grip on the Glock and did as ordered. Karzan stepped behind him and reached around his waist to remove the pistol from his belt.

Karzan stuffed the pistol into his waistband and said, "Nice Glock."

Farhood was indignant. "What are you doing? I told you who this is."

"And how do we know you've not been compromised and are now working for the *Pasdaran*[13] and brought one of them to this meeting? Your friend looks like an Iranian, and his Farsi is pretty damned good."

"My friend," said Michael, keeping his hands palms down on the table, "If I were with the *Pasdaran* you would likely already be dead or on your way to Evin Prison. I assume you have men on the street who would have warned you if we had not come alone. The fact that you were waiting for us in this apartment suggests that

---

[13] Iranian Revolutionary Guard Corps

your men saw nothing suspicious. I arrived in the country at Mehrabad airport several days ago. I doubt the *Pasdaran* would go to such lengths."

After asking permission, he gingerly pulled his plane ticket and old boarding pass from an inside pocket, along with the Spanish passport. Placing them on the table in front of Karzan, he said, "And, yes, my parents were Iranian, but I was born in Tel Aviv."

Karzan examined the documents, especially the passport. "This does not say your name is Barid."

"And my real name is not Barid, either," said Michael. "My real name is not even the one most people know me by. Did you expect me to have a Star of David tattooed on my forehead?"

Karzan studied Michael with the caution of a man considering buying a used car. "What is your mission here?"

Michael gave him a level stare. "I'm going to kill someone."

"Who?"

"A man we consider dangerous. That's all you need to know."

"When do you plan to do this?"

"As soon as we have an escape plan ready to go. The government will react, probably violently, and we will need to get out of the country. We'll need your help with an exfiltration, if it comes to that."

"You intend to cross the border into Kurdistan?"

"I don't see a viable alternative. If things go smoothly and we get away clean, I may be able to leave the country as I arrived, as a peaceful Spanish merchant. But we can't count on that. We need a back-up plan, and you're the only game in town."

Karzan scratched his chin. He looked from Michael to Farhood and then placed the Glock on the table and slid it across to Michael. "It won't be easy," he said. He looked at the burly man with the Kalashnikov. "What do you think, Sangar?" He turned to the man with the shaved head.

Sangar leaned his rifle against the wall and sat at the table next to Karzan. "If the security forces and the *Basij* are on the warpath it will be touchy," he said in a voice that sounded like gravel hitting metal. "Speed will be essential. You want to get out of Tehran before they have time to react. Even then, there will be patrols on the highways, roadblocks, searches. And it's nearly 700 kilometers to the border. They'll probably suspect we are responsible for the incident, and that will make the border area more dangerous than usual."

"We'll need documents, too," said Michael. "Three sets, for me, Farhood, and his sister. Can you provide them?"

"Yes," said Karzan, "but it will take a day or two, and we'll need photos."

"I suggest we meet here again tomorrow night," said Michael, "to review the plan."

CHAPTER 18

Thursday morning - the day before the Islamic day of congregational prayer and worship.

Snow began to fall Wednesday evening and continued through the night, leaving Tehran veiled in white. But the streets were being cleared, and traffic was flowing, though more slowly than usual.

Time was running out. Michael had been in Tehran for over a week, and his Spanish persona had to all intents and purposes disappeared, something which might well have come to the attention of the authorities.

Grim faced, he and Farhood dressed warmly in hooded winter jackets and motorcycle helmets that hid their faces. They left the apartment building on the motorbike with Farhood driving and Michael on the rear seat. Over one shoulder he carried a bag containing the object that had been in the package delivered by Karzan.

The Science and Technology building where Asadi worked was over eight kilometers from the apartment over still slippery, but negotiable streets. They gave themselves over an hour to navigate the route. Seriyah left fifteen minutes after them in the Toyota. She would take up a position a short distance from the site of the planned action, where Michael and Farhood would dump the motorbike and switch to the car.

Shaykh Bahay was an attractive, tree-lined street that was home to many mid-sized businesses. The neighborhood was laid out in a regular grid of straight streets. To the west the area was bounded by a busy highway with limited access, making it unsuitable to escape in that direction. A few blocks east was a major thoroughfare that would take them south, back toward the District 8 safehouse. There were no narrow, dark alleys into which to escape which made timing all the more important.

They had three blocks in which to mount the operation. After Asadi's car turned north from Molla Sadra into Shaykh Bahay Street he had to traverse a long, straight stretch before reaching the turn toward his office.

Waiting in the slush between parked cars they watched as Asadi's Mercedes slowly turned into the street, carefully navigating the slick patches. The sun was rising into a now clear, light blue winter sky and glinted off the plate glass windows of the high-rise buildings.

Farhood gunned the motorbike to bring it alongside the Mercedes as Michael extracted a round, metallic object from the bag. As soon as they were alongside the car, he slapped the magnetized object onto the rear door. Asadi was in the rear seat and looked up in surprise at the thump on his door, thinking they had hit something. But he saw nothing, only a motorbike with two riders surging ahead. He assumed the bike had bumped into the car.

Michael had set the explosive charge to detonate five seconds after the magnet was attached, time enough for them to get clear, but not enough for the target to react.

They were well ahead of the Mercedes when the device exploded with a roar that broke windows, destroying the Mercedes and sending its burning hulk careening across the street where it collided with other cars. Chunks of shrapnel fell all around them as the peaceful street was turned into chaos filled with black smoke and flames. Half a block ahead lay their escape route, a right turn into a side street where Seriyah waited with the Toyota.

Farhood was charged with adrenaline, eyes wild inside the helmet and his body tingling with electricity. Time seemed to have slowed down, and all he could feel was the overpowering urge to escape. His body tensed as he gripped the handlebars and gunned the engine. The bike gained speed – too much speed, and the turn came up faster than he expected. He turned the wheel and squeezed the handbrake, and the bike skidded on the slick street, the wheels sliding out from under them and crashing on its side.

Michael managed to jump clear, but Farhood stayed with the bike as it slid on its side. Finally, its wheels wedged underneath a parked car and trapped his leg beneath it.

Michael rolled heavily over the hard surface of the street, cursing Farhood's amateurism. All the Iranian had to do was drive normally, and their escape would have been a piece of cake. Disaster now loomed.

He picked himself up and rushed over to Farhood who was struggling futilely to free himself. His lower leg was wedged tightly under the crashed bike and the car. He'd removed his helmet, and his face was contorted with pain and fear. "I think my leg is broken," he gasped between clinched teeth. "I can't get out of here."

Looking back over his shoulder Michael could see a crowd gathering in the street behind them, surrounding the burning vehicles. There was a lot of shouting, and he could hear sirens in the distance. Within minutes the area would be swarming with police, and he could not afford to remain there.

He gave a tentative tug to the bike and then pulled harder, but it would not budge. There was no choice. "Farhood, listen to me. I can't stay here, and you can't get out. Police will be here shortly. Tell them you were startled by the explosion and lost control of the bike. Given the general chaos, that will be believable. They should get you out and give you medical attention. Then you can meet Seriyah and me back at the safehouse. Can you do that?"

Farhood was frightened, but he said, "Go, go. I'll be OK."

Michael squeezed the young man's shoulder and then sprinted down the street where Seriyah should be waiting with the Toyota. It was imperative that they clear the area immediately.

He spotted the car parked half-way down the block with its engine running and piled into the passenger seat.

"Where is Farhood?" asked Seriyah as she cast anxious glances in all directions.

"There was an accident with the bike, and he's injured. He couldn't make it. We have to leave – now!"

"I won't leave without Farhood." She started to

open her door, but Michael grabbed her arm.

"He's injured and can't move, Seriyah. He should be OK, though, and he'll come back to the apartment as soon as he's able. But right now, we have to get out of here or we'll all end up in prison."

Tears coursed down her cheeks as she cast him a desperate glance. "But they'll arrest him."

"There's no reason to believe that. He's just a guy who crashed his bike because he was scared by the explosion. I'm sure there are lots of other people in the same situation. He shouldn't come under any suspicion. Now, get us out of here."

The harsh tone of his voice startled her into action. She put the car into gear and pulled into the street. Behind them Shaykh Bahay Street was filling with police cars, blue lights flashing. An ambulance flashed past them as they drove away.

CHAPTER 19

Back at the apartment in District 8, Michael and Seriyah gratefully closed the door behind them. The drive back in the nondescript Toyota had been entirely uneventful, but Seriyah's anxiety for her brother did not abate.

"As long as he plays the role of an innocent by-stander, he'll be alright," repeated Michael for what seemed the hundredth time. "There was nothing to be done but leave him there. I could not lift that car off him. They'll take him to a hospital and then release him."

Right now, Michael was more concerned about the next step – his escape from Iran. He had a rendezvous with Karzan and his friend after dark that evening.

Seriyah removed her *hijab* and coat. Underneath, she wore tight jeans and a heavy, dark sweater. Shoved into her waistband was one of the Glocks from the cache.

"What the hell is that?" Michael stared at the weapon.

"We weren't going out this morning unarmed," she said defiantly. "You're carrying a gun, aren't you?"

"Yes," he said. A sick feeling grew in the pit of his

stomach. "Now, please tell me that Farhood was not packing, too."

She gasped as the realization washed over her like a wave of icy water, and she raised a hand to her mouth. 'Oh, my God. He was, and if they find it ..." Her habitual defiance melted away, and her whole body seemed to sag. Michael was afraid she would collapse and put his arms around her to prevent her falling.

"Seriyah," he said, "I'm afraid we have no choice now. We've got to get out of here. We'll lay low and meet Karzan tonight."

She raised a suddenly tear-stained face to his. "I won't leave without my brother. Maybe he got rid of the gun. Maybe they didn't find it."

"You're grasping at straws, Seriyah. In this business relying on hope is not an option. You must deal with facts. It's just too dangerous to wait."

She was suddenly angry. "Then you go," she spit out the words. "I'll wait here for Farhood if you're so afraid."

Michael was tempted to leave her. Making his way to the border would be much less complicated if he were to go alone.

"Seriyah," he said, "we're burning minutes we may not have arguing." He calculated the time since the operation. The drive back to the safehouse had taken at least a half-hour. What was worse, he realized, was that this was not a safehouse in the normal sense. It was not some anonymous, neutral location, but rather was where Farhood and Seriyah lived. If Farhood had been arrested, his identity documents would reveal his address. "Time is running out," he finished.

"We should wait," she insisted.

"Listen, Seriyah, if Farhood is in custody, his papers will put him at this address. We have to go, now - put some distance between us and this place. Get whatever you need while I pack some things from the cache. We have a long, difficult journey ahead."

She hesitated.

"Look," he reasoned, a sense of urgency overcoming him, "if Farhood is OK, we'll know soon enough. But we need to wait in a safe place until we can be sure. Now, please, do as I ask. If you don't, I'll be forced to leave you here."

"You promise to wait and see?"

"Yes, yes, I promise. Now, for God's sake will you hurry and do what I asked?"

Reassured, she headed for her bedroom while Michael rushed to the cache. He extracted all the money and ammunition he could stuff into his bag."

Minutes later he rejoined Seriyah in the living room. Time was passing much too quickly, time they didn't have. The sound of sirens drew him to the window, and he froze at what he saw.

A police van and two unmarked cars had pulled up in front of the building, and armed men were pouring out heading for the entrance, the only entrance to the building. There would be no escape that way.

"Seriyah, we have a problem. The authorities are here, and they're on their way to this apartment. We have to go."

Her face went white with shock, and she stood frozen to the spot. She wanted to scream but couldn't. Her brother, Farhood, must have been detained. All hope was lost. Her life was at an end. She would kill herself before returning to Evin Prison.

Michael grabbed her by the shoulders and shook her hard. "Snap out of it. We have to move. Wait here a second." He rushed back to the cache and grabbed some hand grenades, hoping they were still functional after their decade-long sleep.

Back in the living room he shoved Seriyah out the door onto the landing. There was a commotion below as the police scrambled up the stairs. Looking over the railing he saw they were already on the second-floor landing.

"Seriyah, go up the stairs, all the way to the top." He pushed her up the steps and turned back as he pulled the pin on a grenade and let it cook off for a few sections. He flicked the it down the stairs and stepped back against the wall. An explosion roared through the stairwell, and the steel shrapnel from the grenade tore into the front rank of the attackers, sending those behind tumbling down. For good measure he tossed another grenade over the railing, aiming for the stairs below with equal effect. Certain the attack had been stymied for the moment, he ran up the stairs after Seriyah.

He found her at the top of the stairwell at a door that must lead to the roof. The door was locked, but he put his shoulder to it, and it gave way. Behind the door was a narrow, dark stairway leading upward. "Follow me," he said. At the top was another door which opened onto the roof.

The medium-rise apartment buildings on this street were spaced closely together, with one roof adjoining another. He led Seriyah across four neighboring rooftops until they could go no further. The utility door on this roof presented no problem, and they were soon clambering down the stairs to street level. Fortunately, this building's entrance faced a different street.

From around the corner in the direction of the safehouse the air was filled with a cacophony of klaxons and sirens and men shouting. Thick smoke hung over the street, and a fire engine screamed around the corner in front of them.

Motioning for Seriyah to follow, he stepped into the street and began walking in the opposite direction fighting the desire to run.

"We need to get out of this area fast, Seriyah. What do you suggest?"

Still in shock, it took a moment for her to respond. "There's a subway station near Golbarg Street."

The snow was still fresh on the sidewalks, crunching under their feet, and the air was crisp. Michael was dressed warmly in a padded jacket and knit cap, the leather bag containing the items recovered from the cache over his shoulder, and Seriyah wore a long coat and a woolen scarf covered her head.

Emergency vehicles continued to pass them as they made their way to the underground metro station. Seriyah bought two tickets and they boarded a train heading south. They changed trains at Imam Khomeini Station to take the line heading west.

The rendezvous with Karzan was not until after dark, and it was still well before noon. "We need to find a place where we can spend some time, maybe a café, but in a residential area. Any ideas?"

Seriyah was slowly recovering from her initial shock, though she was still distraught about Farhood.

"Maybe the Sarif University area. There's a metro station there and plenty of shops and cafes."

"Good girl."

They emerged onto a busy, four-lane street lined with apartment buildings and small shops and cafes. The sun was rising higher into the sky, and some of the snow had begun to melt, making the sidewalks slushy. Michael selected a café, and they stepped inside.

The morning's exertions had given Michael an appetite, and he suspected there would not be many decent meals in the days to come. He ordered hot coffee and rice and lamb stew. Seriyah ordered sweet tea and feta cheese with a dollop of jam atop some Lavash bread.

Michael tucked into his stew and cast a critical eye at Seriyah's plate. "You need to eat. We have a long, hard road ahead if we're to survive. There's not much sustenance on your plate."

"I doubt I can choke anything down right now," she said, sipping the hot tea. All I can think about is Farhood."

"I understand. It's a tragedy. But we all knew going in that it was a dangerous thing we were doing, and yet we went ahead, and the operation was a success. Farhood is a hero, and that is something you must always remember."

"You don't understand what being arrested in Iran means." She shivered, and her eyes again filled with tears. "You can't imagine the depravity, the torture, the degradation. And in the end, all that awaits is to be put against a wall and shot. I have seen this firsthand, and it's all I can think about now."

"Seriyah, our first concern right now is to escape

Iran. If we do, at least Farhood's sacrifice will not have been in vain. It won't diminish your pain. That will always be with you, but Farhood would want you to escape, to be free."

She looked at him straight in the face, her eyes soft with tears, "I will tell you something, Barid. I will never allow myself to be captured. I still have the pistol, and if I must, I will use it on myself before I let them take me."

"I believe you, Seriyah."

CHAPTER 20

Something he did not mention to Seriyah worried Michael. Farhood would be subjected to savage torture, and Farhood knew their escape plan. What was worse, he knew Karzan's identity. Unfortunately, escape across the border was their only option. The Azerbaijan border was even more distant. It was reasonable to assume that the Iranians would figure this out, with or without Farhood telling them.

Using his Spanish passport was out of the question, too, given the circumstances, and it would do Seriyah no good in any event. If Farhood had broken, the Iranians would have his description. Undoubtedly, they knew that Seriyah was his sister.

A bright spot was that Karzan had come through with the false identity documents that identified him and Seriyah as husband and wife. The documents might get them through some checkpoints, but he expected to have to pass through a gauntlet of security between Tehran and the border. The Iranians would pull out all the stops to capture them. He had to accept the likelihood that he and the girl would end up in unmarked graves.

That Seriyah was strong and determined he had no doubt. But she had no combat skills, had never even fired a weapon. He would be better off on his own, but he resolved not to abandon her. There was something about this tragic girl that drew him to her. And she trusted him, and trust was a precious thing.

They lingered over their meal for over an hour before venturing back onto the street. Considering what lay ahead of them, Michael said, "We need to find some more suitable clothing. We're going to be passing through some very rough terrain in the next few days, and what you're wearing won't do, especially up in the mountains."

They searched along the street until they found a shop that displayed camping gear and rugged clothing in the window. The shop was empty except for the proprietor who was more than pleased to see them begin to stack items on the counter. Boots, heavy clothing, and sleeping bags. All the equipment was French-made, which pleased Michael. There was even a selection of survival rations. They packed everything into a backpack which Michael hoisted easily over one shoulder. A smaller pack for Seriyah was stuffed into it, as well.

When it came time to pay, Michael lay some crisp one-hundred-dollar bills on the counter. There were no problems spending U.S. dollars or euros in Iran. The country needed all the hard currency it could get, even those printed by the Great Satan.

Back on the street, Michael said, "We still have to find a place to stay until dark." After some searching, they found a small hotel and checked in as husband and wife. Their identity documents said they were from a small city northwest of Tehran called Zanjan. Michael checked them in for three days and paid in advance with more dollars.

The room was modest, but it contained a double bed into which he immediately tumbled. "Come on and lie down, Seriyah. This might be the last bed you see for a while."

The girl was shocked. "You want me to get into bed with you?"

"I won't bite, and we both need the rest. I can sleep on the floor, if you prefer."

She hesitated a beat, then said, "No, don't do that. You're right. We need to rest."

She lay down beside him in the narrow bed. Anxiety had taken its toll and left her more exhausted than she realized. She was asleep almost immediately.

Michael lay on his back considering the many ways things still could go wrong. He tried hard not to be pessimistic, but the odds were stacked heavily against them.

CHAPTER 21

Michael lay for hours, unable to sleep, listening to Seriyah's soft breathing beside him. Tonight's meeting with Karzan was by no means certain or without danger. The appearance of the security services at the apartment safehouse so quickly confirmed beyond doubt that Farhood had been identified as part of the assassination team. The apartment address had been gleaned from Farhood's identity documents. But Farhood also knew the location of the safehouse where they'd met with Karzan. By now, he had been in custody for many hours. The question was whether the young Iranian had been able to hold out. That he was being tortured was beyond doubt, and he already had a serious injury which the authorities were sure to exploit. No matter what people who had never experienced it thought, torture is effective.

Finally, the light faded outside the hotel room window. He gently shook Seriyah's shoulder. "It's time," he said.

She came awake slowly and stared at his face for a long moment. "Yes. I'm ready."

He checked their equipment once again, by force of habit removing the magazine from his pistol and working the slide to eject the extra round in the chamber, then reloading. He then did the same with Seriyah's pistol before handing it to her. "There's a round in the chamber and seventeen more in the magazine. All you need to do is point and shoot. There's no need to release a safety on a Glock. Put it in your belt or coat pocket where you can reach it easily."

"Are you expecting more trouble?"

"It's always possible. We have to be ready for the unexpected."

"You're worried that Farhood has revealed the location of Karzan's safehouse, aren't you?"

"It's a possibility."

"Farhood will resist them. He is brave."

"I don't doubt his courage, but we have to be realistic."

Her lips trembled as she spoke. "This is not his first experience with torture. He won't tell them anything."

"I hope you're right," said Michael.

Her dark eyes flashed. "My brother is going to die. He knows that no matter what he says, the end will be the same. He will protect us." Large, oily tears suddenly rolled down her cheeks, and Michael wanted to embrace her, but he didn't know how she would react. This girl who had greeted him so bravely only a few days earlier with a pistol pointed at his chest now seemed small and fragile. There was nothing he could say that would soften the harsh reality of her brother's predicament.

"Put on your coat. It's time to leave," he said.

He slung his leather bag over one shoulder and the pack over the other. Only the desk clerk was in the lobby, and he paid them scant attention. Michael had feared that leaving the hotel with all the bags would raise suspicion, but he had paid for the room for three days in advance, and the clerk couldn't have cared less what they were carrying.

Out on the street Michael led them quickly away from the hotel and onto a side street. Seriyah was mystified. "What are you doing?"

"We're going to steal a car," he replied, stopping beside a vintage Nissan sedan. "I don't recall a Metro station near Karzan's place, and I don't want to get trapped underground in any event. The authorities know who you are, and there is probably an all-points bulletin out to police to be on the look-out for you. Taxis are insecure. So, we'll steal a car and drive there ourselves."

He checked one of the Nissan's doors and found it unlocked. "Now, there's a piece of luck, at last," he said, hoping this was a good sign. He bundled Seriyah into the passenger seat and tossed the pack into the back, keeping the leather bag with the remaining grenades, money, and ammunition at his side. It took only seconds to start the car and drive away.

"You're going to have to give me directions," he said. "Farhood drove to the first meeting."

Karzan's safehouse was in the southern section of the city in a poor neighborhood. In this area, unlike the affluent north, women wore *chadors* on the street. The mullahs were popular here. But regardless of religious loyalties, the streets here were dangerous with roaming bands of thugs, thieves, and drug addicts. Karzan knew how to choose his cover.

He cruised past the rundown apartment building where the safehouse was located, scanning the surroundings for hostile indicators, cars that seemed out of place, suspicious loiterers.

His task was made more difficult by the fact that there were groups of young men hanging on street corners the way they did all over the world in poor, crime-ridden neighborhoods, hyenas hoping for an easy kill.

A light shone from the window of Karzan's safehouse - the agreed upon safety signal. So far, so good, he thought. The Kurd's big truck with an enclosed bed was parked in front. The building was in the middle of the block, and parking was haphazard. In a neighborhood where automobile ownership was too expensive for most residents, Michael had no trouble finding a spot only a short distance from the building entrance.

This was the most dangerous moment – entering the building and going to the apartment. An ambush could be waiting inside, careful planning ensuring that no trace of the authorities' presence would be visible outside. Entering required an act of faith, something the careful operative in Michael abhorred. Thus far today, their escape had been clean, or at least appeared to have been. Inside the building lay either salvation or peril. But in this instance, there was no choice. The way out of Iran lay with Karzan.

They made their way quickly to the entrance, Michael already with gun in hand. He placed Seriyah behind him and taking a deep breath pushed open the door.

Nothing. The gloom inside was broken only by a single bare bulb dangling from the ceiling just inside the door. Likewise, the stairs were illuminated by a single bulb at each landing. Keeping Seriyah behind him with his pistol in the ready position, Michael ascended the stairs to the fourth floor. Lowering the backpack onto the floor, he knocked on the safehouse door – two long, one short.

After a moment, the door opened slowly. Karzan's big, bearded friend stood in the middle of the room, his Kashnikov pointed at the doorway. Karzan had stepped aside out of the line of fire, but when he recognized Michael and Seriyah, he signaled them inside and closed the door quickly behind them. "I wasn't sure you would come. The police are looking for you everywhere. Another ten minutes, and we would have been gone."

"We're grateful you waited. We're ready," said Michael, "and we can't leave soon enough."

"Agreed," said Karzan. "What happened?"

"There was an accident. Farhood was injured and captured. They raided his apartment this morning, and we barely managed to get away."

"That's bad. Our man in the police says they have the girl's description and know that another man is involved."

Michael was frankly surprised that Karzan had not simply abandoned them. He must know as well as Michael that Farhood could betray the location of the safehouse. The fact that the Kurd had a source in the police was another pleasant surprise. "I wouldn't have blamed you if you'd left, Karzan."

"Well," said the Kurd with a sly grin, "I had some insurance."

"Your plant in the police?"

"Yes, him ... and my three men in the building across the street with Kalashnikovs."

Michael grinned back at him. "Karzan, if you weren't so ugly, I'd kiss you."

"For the first time in my life, I thank my mother that I'm ugly. Still, I don't want to stay here any longer. We need to go, now."

Five minutes later, Michael sat in the truck beside Karzan. The big Kurd had given Michael a heavy woolen sweater that boasted several ragged holes, an old army field jacket, and a wool cap that he pulled down over his ears. Michael's beard had grown over the past several days, and he looked more Iranian than ever. Karzan looked him up and down before boarding the truck. "Good. Now you look like you belong here."

Seriyah was concealed in the back behind some crates, wrapped in blankets and buried under a stack of gunny sacks.

The truck rumbled through the streets of Tehran in the direction of the Alborz Mountains.

CHAPTER 22

It was nearly 650 kilometers from Tehran to Marivan in Kurdistan Province if one took the main toll road leading away from the city. The village lay almost directly west of Tehran.

But Karzan chose a different direction in favor of a less travelled route. "This will take more time," he said over the roar of the old truck's engine, "but we'll run into fewer patrols and check-points. They're looking for a man and a woman traveling together, so with some luck we should get through everything but a thorough search of the truck. Just look stupid and give them your papers when they ask for them."

"With luck, we might avoid being stopped altogether, but I don't believe in luck." Michael gripped the Glock-17 in his jacket pocket. "Is there a way to avoid built-up areas and villages?"

Karzan grunted his response. "We'll turn off the main road well before we reach Qazvin and stick to secondary roads and trails. It's a big, fairly empty area, and once we cross into Kordestan Province our security will be a little better. It depends on how badly they want to catch you. Judging from what I hear, they want you very, very much. And they have a lot of resources. They may bring in the military. It'll get hairy if they do."

"Nothing good has happened since I arrived in this country," grumbled Michael as he stared out the window at the passing countryside. "When do you think we'll reach Marivan?"

Karzan snorted. "Oh, it'll take us a few days with all the snow. This truck runs well, and the tires are new, but she's old, and the back roads will slow us down. We'll have to find a place to shelter before dawn. They'll probably send out helicopters as soon as it's light, and I don't want to be moving on the road."

They headed away from Tehran northwest toward the town of Qazvin. The dark road passed through a long valley with several new industrial sites on the outskirts of Tehran. The road was good and macadamed. Karzan settled the truck into a steady 70 kilometers-per-hour, and soon they were passing agricultural fields and a few small farming villages. On the right loomed the dark hulk of the Alborz mountain range, a jagged shadow against a clear night sky. Some peaks rose to over 18,000 feet. On the other side of the mountains lay the Caspian Sea. When the snow melted in the spring, water would cascade down the mountains to fill dry stream beds and irrigate thirsty crops.

By midnight they'd been on the road for over two hours and had run into only one check-point about thirty kilometers outside the city. It was manned by two uniformed police officers who did not appear to be pleased to have been called to duty at such an hour. One checked their papers and flashed a light into the truck's cab while the other circled them. Michael tensed and put his hand on his pistol when the cop lifted the canvas at the back of the truck and shined his flashlight inside. But the soldier saw only a load of wooden crates and lost interest. Nevertheless, cold sweat poured down Michael's back as they pulled away. He could only imagine what Seriyah was feeling.

The truck had no heater, and Michael hugged himself to keep warm, wishing he had a pair of gloves. Karzan turned off the main road onto a dirt path before reaching the outskirts of Qazvin. They jolted in and out of ruts with bone cracking ferocity as Karzan fought the steering wheel against the ice and snow. No matter how tough the Kurdish warrior was, Michael thought he must be exhausted. But the man remained grimly calm as he navigated through the night.

Around them the moon illuminated barren, snow-covered terrain and deep ravines. The dirt roads were treacherous, and the old truck's weak headlights barely showed the way ahead. Michael hoped Karzan knew the route; otherwise disaster was but an instant away.

After what seemed like hours, Karzan said, "We'll get back onto a main road soon, and then it's only a few kilometers to a place we can stay," he said, sensing Michael's unease. "It's an old truck stop with a shop selling groceries and fuel. I know the owner, and he'll let us rest there for a day. I'll tell him we've been driving all night and just need to sleep and get some food. We can't let anyone see Seriyah, though. There is an empty warehouse. I'll park inside so she can stretch her legs. Other than that, she stays in the truck."

"How much farther after that to Marivan?"

"It's still a good distance over these roads. No way we can make it overnight, but at least we'll get into Kordestan Province. I'll find a phone and call for some back-up then."

The truck stop turned out to be a long, low ramshackle building with a tin roof that sat astride a dusty crossroads. There were two fuel pumps in front that looked as though they should be in a museum exhibit. The sun was just coming up when they arrived. A thin old man wearing a heavy padded jacket, a knit cap, and a muffler that covered half his face already was setting out signs advertising the delights offered inside the shop.

"That's old Rashid," said Karzan. "He's not changed in decades."

"Do you trust him?"

"Are you crazy? Of course, I don't trust him. He's a thieving old bastard who'll try to cheat you out of your shoes, and he's Iranian, and his wife is Afghan. I'll go see if we can park in the warehouse and get some breakfast."

The old man gave Karzan a nearly toothless grin as he approached, and there was much arm waving as they talked.

The old man went back inside, and Karzan walked back to the truck. "We can park in the warehouse. Rashid is rousting his wife to make some breakfast for us. I told him we were really hungry."

"Was he suspicious?"

"He couldn't understand why we had driven all night, but I told him I was hauling some perishables. I don't think we should stay here all day, though, so we'll get a couple of hours sleep and be on our way. It's a risk traveling by day, but if the old man gets too curious, it could be a problem."

The warehouse had seen better days and looked

even worse inside than outside. The ceiling was supported by heavy timbers, and the floor was dirt. Various rusting automobile and truck parts were strewn about the place. There was no door, so the building did little to keep out the biting cold.

Karzan went to the main building and returned with an iron pot and a stack of naan bread. Seriyah clambered out of the truck shaking with cold.

"Why don't you change into the warm clothing we bought in Tehran. We still have a long way to go," Michael told her. He lugged the backpack out of the truck and started pulling out the clothing they'd bought for her.

She bundled everything in her arms and went looking for a dark corner where she could change. When she returned wearing heavy pants, a thick sweater and a military style jacket, Michael looked her over and said, "Put on the knit cap and pull it down over your ears. Make sure all your hair is covered." She did this, and Michael nodded in satisfaction. "You could pass for a boy if needs be," he said.

Karzan had placed the steaming pot on the floor and removed its cloth cover. The meaty aroma was overpowering, and Michael realized he was hungry. He looked into the pot and was startled to see a sheep's head staring back at him.

Karzan passed the naan around. "It's *kalah pacha*," he said. "It'll make you strong. It's an Afghan dish. Just pick the meat off the bone and soak up the liquid with the naan. It's the perfect breakfast for a cold morning."

They picked the meat with their fingers, and soon Michael was enjoying the dish. It was savory and well spiced, and the broth was fortifying. Michael wished there were coffee, but Karzan had brought only a thermos of sweet tea.

"That old bastard, Rashid, charged an arm and a leg for this," said Karzan as he picked up the iron pot to carry it back to the main building. I'll get a few more things for the road. We should get what rest we can now. I don't want to stay here for more than a few hours."

"You'd better sleep, Karzan," said Michael. "You've done all the work so far. You, too, Seriyah. We still have a long way to go. I'll keep watch."

He didn't have to convince the Kurd, who spread some blankets from the back of the truck on the floor and soon dropped deeply into sleep, if the strength of his snoring was any indicator.

Seriyah sat leaning against one of the truck's wheels, eyes downcast and arms around her knees.

"You should get some rest, too," said Michael.

"I can't sleep. Too much has happened."

"Seriyah ..."

"Don't try to comfort me. Nothing can bring me comfort except for a thousand mullahs hanging from lampposts. Hatred will sustain me now."

"We'll get out of this. We're already half-way to the border. You'll be able to start a new life away from all of this."

She pierced him with a sharp stare. "I don't want a new life. I want revenge. I want to kill them."

"I know." It was all he could say. He understood anger and hatred. He felt it for his country's enemies who had made a profession of murdering innocents. This beautiful young girl was infused with the same animus toward those who had locked her country and her people into a medieval world of ignorance and intolerance. Senseless hatred had become the driving force of Iran, the eternal "us" versus "them," dragging proud Persians into a cesspool churning with xenophobia and ignorance. A nation once renowned for its contributions to civilization had reverted to the Dark Ages as the world stood by aghast but powerless. Even the old Shah, for all his faults and the abuses of his *Savak*[14] could be pitied. That the Americans had withdrawn their support from him at a critical moment in favor of a "popular" revolution was a mistake that would reverberate through the ages.

"You'd better get some sleep, too," said Seriyah. "I can't."

He crawled into the back of the truck and lay on the gunny sacks and blankets behind the crates. Despite the turmoil of his thoughts, exhaustion took over, and he was soon asleep.

---

[14] *Savak* – The Shah's secret police.

CHAPTER 23

Michael was instantly awake but could not at first determine what had disturbed him. He sat up, listening, and then heard it – the unmistakable distant thwack of helicopter blades cutting into the thin, mountain air.

He leapt out of the truck and found Karzan standing at the warehouse entrance looking into the sky. Seriyah was beside him staring wide-eyed over his shoulder.

The sound grew louder and within seconds they spotted a black dot on the horizon that quickly became larger. Michael recognized the outline of an old Soviet MI-8, an alarming sight because besides its crew of three, the MI-8 could serve as a troop carrier and could be equipped with an array of armaments. If it landed and a squad of soldiers with automatic weapons jumped out, it would all be over for them.

They backed into the frigid shadow of the interior and waited as the helicopter approached and circled overhead, a few thousand feet above them. A moment passed, and the ship moved on. Michael was grateful for Karzan's foresight in moving the truck inside the warehouse.

No one said a word for a few moments as the

implications sank in.

Still squinting in the direction of the receding helicopter, the big Kurd said, "They know where we're headed. I think we can expect problems ahead."

Michael agreed. "I'm worried about that road check we passed through outside Tehran. Those guys, as incompetent as they were, might have reported it, so they would have a description of the truck leaving the city not long after the assassination."

"It's possible. Or Farhood has been forced to talk." Before Seriyah could object, Karzan said, "My dear, no one is immune to torture. Sooner or later, everyone breaks. It's no sign of disrespect to think so. We must be realistic."

Seriyah bit her lip, but stubbornly shook her head.

"It doesn't matter," said Michael. "We have no choice but to go on"

Karzan stroked his beard. "They'll probably have checkpoints on all the main roads. We'll stick to the tracks through the ravines until we have no choice but to come into the open. With a little luck they won't be able to spot us from the air in the deep shadows."

A half-hour later they were on a treacherous path between steep rocky escarpments. In the night, Michael had not appreciated the nature of the terrain. They passed outcroppings of shale, basalt, sandstone, and striated granite. But as they travelled further west into Zanjan Province, the rocks gave way to broad swaths of farmland crisscrossed by myriad secondary and tertiary roads. Though the mass of the Alborz Mountains still dominated the northern horizon, they were now traveling in open country. The protection of the cliffs and ravines was left behind.

"We'll get back into the mountains soon enough, but for now, we're exposed," said Karzan.

They'd decided to let Seriyah ride up front with them, for which she was grateful. She was glad of the warm clothing as the cab was as icy cold as the rear of the truck, but at least she could see something besides the canvas stretched over the metal ribs of the truck bed.

With some trepidation, they constantly scanned the skies. There was traffic even on these back roads, and there was the hope that they would blend in. They did spot helicopters high in the sky on a few occasions, but they did not descend. Whatever they saw, thought Michael, they likely would radio ahead to checkpoints. He exchanged a glance with a grim-visaged Karzan and knew that the big Kurd shared his thoughts. Their luck couldn't hold out forever.

Seriyah sat wordless and brooding between them, staring straight ahead. Michael felt responsible for her. Farhood's fate had affected her strongly, but her reservoir of hatred suggested something deeper and older.

His training had taught him to treat agents objectively, and there were many professional intelligence officers who considered agents as mere pawns, the means to an end. Real professionals, some believed abhor personal relationships with agents. To become a Mossad operative was to become a part of something greater than oneself, dedicated to the defense of Israel above all other considerations.

But weren't there considerations even greater than this? How about simple human values? Michael secrctly prided himself for treating agents as human beings. It was too easy to classify such people as mere traitors to their own countries or causes. This was an easy rationalization that permitted sometimes ruthless decisions. Yes, some agents were merely venal bastards, willing to do anything for money, but Michael felt obligated to his agents and their well-being; their very survival depended on his skills as an operative. Yes, hard decisions were unavoidable, but Michael had vowed to himself never to betray an agent.

In fact, Seriyah was not an agent. Both she and Karzan were allies of convenience with their own motivations and objectives. But they were now united in the common objective of escape. There were only two alternatives – escape or death. As a *Kidon* member, he had meted out death to Israel's enemies with sudden brutality, well-planned and carried out with surgical precision. But the assassination of Asadi bore little resemblance to precision, and despite Farhood's carelessness with the motorbike, he could not escape feeling guilty for the youth's capture. It was the Mossad operation that brought on the disaster. Had the mission not brought him to Tehran, Farhood and his sister would still be safe. The young woman beside him would not be fleeing for her life in a desperate and possibly doomed attempt to reach the border. He cursed Eitan Ronan and David Shalev for thrusting him so carelessly into this position.

They were entering more populated zones, and Karzan managed to bypass the town of Zarrin Rood. He found a secondary road that would take them northwest toward Kurdistan. The countryside reacquired some of its rocky, mountainous character interspersed with cultivated fields. Finally, they were forced to take a more travelled route along a macadammed roadway in order to cross a bridge that spanned a deep ravine through which a swift river coursed. Karzan informed them that they would have to pass through several villages and risk checkpoints. The Kurd estimated the trip would take at least another day or two in his ancient truck – with luck. But neither Michael nor Karzan believed in luck.

CHAPTER 24

The good news was that shortly after passing Zarrin Rood, they entered Kordestan, one of Iran's Kurdish provinces. The bad news was that their luck ran out at the village of Garmaab. They managed to circle around the village before rejoining the main road but ran into a road block several kilometers farther west.

"Clever bastards," said Michael. "They set up where there was no alternative route."

"These guys are military," said Karzan, "not police."

In a large country with hundreds of roads, it is not possible to set up heavily manned checkpoints everywhere, especially on secondary roads. A large search area requires disbursement of manpower to cover the most area possible. Thus, the roadblock consisted of a military vehicle that looked like an oversized Jeep with a covered cab, and three uniformed men. It was a cold day, and the soldiers were stamping the ground in an attempt to keep warm.

There was no other traffic to divide the soldiers' attention, so the truck provided a welcome diversion from the boredom of their post. As they drew to a stop, Michael could see that there were two enlisted men and one officer. The enlisted men had Kalashnikov's slung over their shoulders, and the officer carried what looked like a Heckler & Koch MP5 submachinegun.

Karzan drew the truck to a creaky, groaning halt and waited. The officer climbed onto the running board and tapped on the window with the barrel of his gun. Karzan obligingly rolled down the window, and the officer scrutinized the three people in the cab.

"Where are you going?" he asked.

Karzan adopted a placating demeanor. "*Salam baradar.*[15] We are headed for Bijar."

"Why are you on this road?"

Karzan jerked his head in Michael's direction. "My friend here is from Qazvin, *baradar.* We stopped there to visit his family."

The lieutenant hopped off the running board and gestured with his weapon. "Out of the truck. All of you."

With a glance at Michael, Karzan climbed down from the cab while Michael and Seriyah did the same on the other side. He hid his pistol under the seat.

The two soldiers had unlimbered their Kalashnikovs. Desperately trying to improvise a plan, Michael led Seriyah to the rear of the truck, which upset the lieutenant. "Seriyah, stay here out of sight as long as possible," and he hurried around the truck to join Karzan and the lieutenant.

"Where is the boy?" asked the lieutenant, squinting toward the back of the truck.

"You scared him," said Michael. He had to take a piss."

"Humph." The lieutenant took their identity

---

[15] Greetings, brother.

documents and instructed the two soldiers to watch Karzan and Michael at the front of the truck.

Michael had hoped to keep all the soldiers together where with some luck he and Karzan could prevail in a close-quarter fight. But they were shoved around to face the truck while the soldiers slung their rifles and started patting them down.

It was an opportunity, perhaps the only one they would get, and Michael tensed his body in preparation to attack, locking eyes with the Kurd to make sure they acted in unison. He looked across the hood of the truck at the lieutenant, gauging whether he could disable the man behind him and still have enough time to reach the officer before he could bring his submachinegun to bear. At best, it was a longshot.

The lieutenant was studying their documents, facing toward the front of the truck. There was movement behind him as Seriyah stepped from behind the truck, her arms held straight in front with the pistol in her hands. She fired as she stepped forward. Over the hood of the truck as if in slow-motion Michael saw the lieutenant stagger as the first 9mm round struck him in the shoulder. He spun around, a look of shock and surprise on his face, and Seriyah continued toward him, firing more rounds. Finally, the lieutenant crumpled to the ground. Seriyah, her weapon still raised, continued her advance toward the wounded man.

All of this happened in mere seconds, and time sped up again. Michael drove an elbow into the soldier behind him and turned to deliver a blow to the man's throat with stiffened fingers. From somewhere Karzan produced a huge knife which he plunged into the belly of the man who'd been searching him. He then grasped the soldier by the hair and slit his throat from ear to ear.

The man Michael had attacked was lying on the ground, hands to his throat, making ghastly gurgling sounds.

More shots rang out. Turning, Michael saw Seriyah pumping more rounds into the lieutenant as he lay at her feet. She emptied the magazine into him, and the look on her face was not one Michael would wish to see again. She continued to pull the trigger, even after the slide locked back.

He rushed to the side of the truck as she began kicking the prostrate body of the lieutenant. "Seriyah, stop. He's dead. It's over."

He put his arms around her. She was trembling violently and nearly hysterical. He dragged her away from the body and held her until the trembling stopped.

Karzan stooped to the soldier Michael had put down and calmly slit his throat. "That will put an end to the dog's suffering," he said. "What do we do now?"

Michael led Seriyah to the back of the truck and told her to wait there. Returning to Karzan, he said, "The first thing is to get rid of these bodies."

They dragged the dead men into the ditch and covered them as best they could with snow and dead brush.

Karzan gave the soldiers' vehicle a speculative look. "We could move a lot faster in that thing."

"Yes," said Michael, "and the first time someone saw three civilians in it, we'd find trouble, especially if we run into another roadblock."

"I don't think we should leave it here, though, so

close to the bodies."

"You're right."

Michael drove the ersatz Jeep several kilometers with the others following in the truck. The idea was to disassociate the vehicle from the location of the bodies. It was a delaying tactic that might just give them some more time.

CHAPTER 25

Tel Aviv

It was three weeks after Michael Mossberg's departure for Tehran, and Eitan Ronan was worried. He'd decided to remain in Israel until the mission was complete, a mission about which he had serious misgivings.

"David, I still think it was a bad idea." Ronan sat in David Shalev's office wishing desperately for a cigarette.

"Maybe it was," replied Shalev, "but we needed to fire a warning shot across the Mullahs' bows, and timing it close to the Russian's assassination in Paris left no time for elaborate planning. It was important. There's no way the Iranians won't get the message."

"And we may have sacrificed a very good officer."

"Yes, that's possible, though I have confidence in Michael's ingenuity. Such decisions are not easy and always carry risk. My job is to send my people into harm's way, and they understand this. If there is a way to buy this country another day of existence, I'll find it, and sometimes the price is high. Of course, I'll likely rot in hell for some of the things I've done."

"Jews don't believe in hell," said Eitan.

"That's what I'm counting on," replied Shalev with no trace of amusement.

Eitan frowned. "At least we know that Asadi is dead." They'd monitored Iranian communications since Mossberg entered the country.

"And that one of the people involved was taken into Iranian custody. We hope it wasn't Michael, but it almost certainly means that his Spanish cover is blown. He won't be flying out of Tehran."

"He would have been back long before now," said Eitan.

"Then the back-up plan has been put into motion, and he's in the hands of our Kurdish friends, the PKK."

Mossad's ties to the Kurds had until recently been a closely held secret, even from the Americans who had long considered the PKK a terrorist organization. But in Israeli eyes, anyone fighting the Turks, the Iraqis, and the Iranians made a useful, if not completely trustworthy ally. The Kurds did not exactly relish working with the Israelis either but did so in exchange for intelligence and some logistical support, especially weapons.

"It's a long way from Tehran to the border with Kurdistan," said Eitan, "and communications intercepts indicate the Iranians are more interested than normal in that area."

"At least it's an indication he's still on the run, and there's nothing that would indicate Michael has been captured. He's on his own for now," sighed Shalev, "and we can only wait. Waiting is always the hardest part."

"I don't like waiting," said Eitan. "I want to go to

Kurdistan."

Shalev blinked at him. "Are you sure, Eitan? It could be dangerous."

Eitan snorted. "Dangerous? Not half as dangerous as the position we put Michael into. No, I want to go as soon as possible. I want to be there when my man crosses the border ... if he crosses the border. The least we owe him is a familiar face to greet him."

Shalev stroked his cheek. "Maybe not such a bad idea. The Kurds may need some encouragement. I'll ask for some American help to infiltrate you. They're protecting Kurdistan from the Iraqis these days. You can come out the same way."

Eitan stepped outside the building and pulled a blue Gauloise packet from his pocket. He extracted a cigarette and lit it, inhaling deeply. The strong, acrid smoke felt good in his lungs and released some of the tension that inhabited his body. With a little clandestine assistance from the Americans, he would get into Iraq and contact the Kurds. Movement, the sense that he was doing something, would be welcome. And though he would never have mentioned it to David Shalev, he vowed that if necessary he would cross into Iran to bring his man out.

CHAPTER 26

Travel was laborious after the incident with the soldiers. They decided to divert once again to less travelled roads, with which Karzan was fortunately familiar. Michael wondered if the Kurd might have smuggling experience. The old truck labored over mountain roads and dirt paths through snow encased farm fields, climbing ever higher. Their speed was reduced to forty kilometers-per-hour by the rugged terrain.

They headed for the ancient city of Bijar, famous for its rugs. Karzan had contacts in the city that could help them. But they didn't drive all the way into the city of 50,000. Instead, Karzan pulled the truck into the yard of a large house made of adobe a few kilometers outside of town. The house was surrounded by a high, mud wall. A burly man who might have been Karzan's twin came out of the house, alerted by their arrival and stared at them suspiciously until Karzan descended to the ground. "Cousin," shouted the man. "This is a surprise."

The two big, nearly identical men embraced and kissed one another on the cheek. "We need a safe place to rest tonight," said Karzan. Turning to Michael, he introduced the man as his cousin, Dimen.

"Welcome," said Dimen. "Welcome to my home."

After they covered the truck with a large tarpaulin, he led them across the courtyard to the house. "Please, come inside. You look like you're freezing."

The house was simple and warm, with thick blue, red, and green rugs covering the floors and some of the walls, adding to the insulation and retaining the warmth generated by the open hearth.

Dimen had a wife and two daughters who rushed to make the visitors comfortable. There was a large pot bubbling on the gas burner of a small stove from which wafted a delicious aroma.

"As usual, cousin, you have perfect timing," said Dimen with a smile. "You're just in time for dinner."

There was a large table near the hearth, and the women began laying out plates and cutlery with a bowl of *dolmen*, grape leaves stuffed with rice and vegetables. The pot on the stove contained *tabit*, a chicken dish with rice and spices.

Dimen's daughters cast curious glances at the two strangers. They were eleven and twelve years old and were astonished when Seriyah removed her knit cap and her long, black hair fell to her shoulders. "You're a girl!" exclaimed the younger one.

Seriyah gave them a tired smile. "I guess I am," she said. "I'd almost forgotten."

Michael complimented the family on the fine rugs that seemed to cover every bare surface in the house and learned that they were the work of Dimen's wife and daughters who wove them on large looms set against the side of the house. Most of what Michael saw here was the result of several years' work and would be sold to help sustain the family.

They were given the opportunity to wash the dust of the road from their skin, and Seriyah even managed a shampoo.

Michael couldn't recall a more satisfying meal. The warm household felt safe and comfortable after their harrowing journey. Dimen had not seemed the least bit curious about why they were there. Michael assumed that he, like his cousin, was a Kurdish nationalist.

Dimen's wife and daughters disappeared into a back room after they cleared the table and put things away in the kitchen. To Michael's delight, their host produced a bottle of Johnny Walker Black Label from a hidden nook and placed glasses on the table. He did not offer any of the scotch to Seriyah but did not object to her remaining with the men.

Michael swallowed the whisky gratefully. He held out his glass for more and was instantly obliged.

"Well, cousin," said Dimen, "what trouble have you brought us now?"

Karzan explained that they were being sought by the authorities and needed to reach Marivan as soon as possible. He asked if Dimen could find them another vehicle, a reliable one that could negotiate the mountain roads. The truck, he said, might be known and would have to remain hidden."

Dimen eyed them dubiously. "You're going for the border, then?"

"Yes," replied Karzan. Nodding in the direction of Michael and Seriyah, he said, "These two have to get across. They have no choice."

Dimen drained his whisky and scratched his beard. "I'll go into town tomorrow and see what I can do. You'll need four-wheel drive where you're going. I can't believe you made it all the way here in that wreck outside."

Karzan was slightly insulted. "It has good tires and a reliable engine. It performed beautifully."

Michael recalled Karzan's white knuckles on the bucking steering wheel as they careened across farm fields and through narrow ravines. It had been the most frightening drive Michael, accustomed to smooth European roadways, had ever experienced. He thought it a miracle they had made it this far.

The bottle emptied, they made arrangements for the night. Karzan would sleep on the floor in the girls' bedroom, and Dimen laid thick comforters and pillows in front of the hearth for Michael and Seriyah. He may have assumed they were together or not, but he made no comment.

Seriyah had been mostly silent throughout the evening, and as he lay beside her wrapped in a comforter and warmed by the embers in the hearth, he sensed she was not asleep.

"What are you thinking about, Seriyah?"

It was a long moment before she answered. "I'm thinking about Farhood, trying to force myself to accept that he is lost forever, and I'll never see him again."

"I have no words to comfort you, and I'm sorry. Soldiers are lost, and Farhood was a soldier. He did his duty and did it bravely. All we can do is cherish the memory of such men and do everything we can to make sure their sacrifices are not in vain."

"I'm frightened, Barid," she whispered.

She used the alias he had given to her and Farhood, and it brought on a pang of guilt. A good operative should always maintain his cover, but she had probably saved his life this day, and he felt he owed her some honesty, something beyond danger and bromides that provided little real comfort. "My name is not Barid," he said, "but I want you to keep calling me that in front of Karzan and the others. My real name is Menashe." Michael had not used his real name since joining the Mossad, but at this moment in time, for this woman, it felt right to do so.

"Menashe," she repeated, rolling the name over her tongue, tasting it, deciding if it was palatable. "Thank you."

"I'm sorry for all of this, Seriyah. I want you to know that."

"Don't be sorry, Menashe. You gave us a chance to strike back, to hurt them. It was something we both desired."

He said nothing and after several minutes, she said, "You don't understand why we feel this way. I suppose there is no way you could possibly understand."

"There are many reasons to hate this regime."

"Yes, there are many reasons, objective reasons, political reasons, but our reasons are personal, more than you can imagine."

"Do you want to talk about it?"

"No, but given the fact that we both might die within the next days or hours, I will tell you." She took some deep breaths, gathering the strength to lay bare her memories. "Do you remember that we told you we had been arrested and imprisoned?"

"Yes."

"They took us to Evin Prison, in the north of Tehran. It's a terrible place, a place no Iranian wants to see because once you go inside those red brick walls, you will never come out. Inside it literally stinks of death and misery. It is a stench one never can get out of one's nostrils. It is a place where screams and moans are the most common sound, as though they are part of the architecture.

"Farhood and I had been caught up in a street demonstration. It was an accident. We were just out shopping, but it made no difference to the police and the *basij*. They rounded us all up, demonstrators, by-standers – everybody. They beat us and forced us onto buses. It was mostly young people, even children.

"We were placed in cells, the boys separated from the girls, and then the beatings and torture began. I knew our uncle would do all he could to secure our release, but it did not come quickly. We were there for days. ... After the beatings came the rapes. There is a belief that all virgins automatically go to heaven, and so the animals who run the prison make sure that there are no virgins in Evin Prison. Even mere girls of twelve or thirteen were raped by gangs of guards." Tears gleamed on her cheeks in the firelight, but her voice remained steady.

"Because of my uncle's efforts, I was placed in solitary confinement, but that did not save me from the rape gangs. The men were filthy and did things to me I cannot bring myself to tell anyone. When they were through, they would punch and kick me, saying horrible things. I didn't think I would survive. In the end, I didn't want to survive.

"I would watch through the bars of my cell as groups of blindfolded girls were marched past, barefoot, in the rags that were left of their clothes. They would lead them outside, line them up against a wall, and shoot them. I could hear the guns. I longed to join them, but it did not happen. In the end, my uncle, by some miracle thanks to contacts in the government, got Farhood and me out. My brother had been tortured terribly. It took us both nearly a year to recover physically and regain some sense of normality. But we could never again really be normal."

Michael was shocked and sickened beyond words. It was one thing to be on the outside and abhor the actions of the Iranian regime, but here was a person who had been inside and helpless to save herself from the unspeakable inhumanity of man to man. All he could say was, "I'm sorry, Seriyah, so sorry." He could understand the rage which had engulfed her when she shot the soldier.

He drew her into his arms, and she did not resist. The wracking sobs finally came as she pressed her face into his shoulder. "We'll get out of here," he whispered, "We'll find a new life for you."

He held her for a long time comforting her until she fell into a fitful sleep. She was exhausted, mentally and physically, and he marveled at her resilience.

CHAPTER 27

Despite a full belly and the whisky, Michael did not sleep well. Seriyah tossed and turned, and he could only imagine the terrors that haunted her dreams.

After a hearty breakfast, Dimen left for the city on his old motorcycle, and all they could do was sit and wait. He finally returned well after noon.

"I found a car for you," he announced as he stepped inside. "One of the brothers has an old Toyota Landcruiser that's in decent shape. He'll bring it around after dark. If you're caught, he'll claim it was stolen."

Outside, thick, dark clouds scudded across a lowering sky threatening more snow, which at this altitude could be thick.

Karzan studied the sky through the window and said, "Well, we can't leave tonight. If it snows, we won't be able to navigate the roads, even with four-wheel drive. That means we don't leave until morning, and we'll have to stick to the main roads all the way."

"How much farther?"

"Around 250 kilometers. We can make it in five or six hours, even with the snow. The main roads should be OK."

The day passed quietly. Karzan decided they should clean their weapons. Unsurprisingly, Dimen possessed everything required to maintain weapons. Karzan had grabbed the officer's submachinegun before they buried the bodies at the roadblock and now laid it on the kitchen table.

"Heckler & Koch," commented Michael. "Nice weapon."

"It's an Iranian version," said Karzan as he disassembled the piece. "They call it an MPT-9. It fires the same ammunition as your Glock-17's. Better at close quarters than my Kalashnikov."

"Let's hope we won't need it," said Michael, which drew a dubious glance and a snort from Karzan.

They made the same sleeping arrangements that night, and Michael and Seriyah settled down by the fire. He lay on his back, thinking of the final leg of their journey and hoping he could sleep. He was surprised when Seriyah moved close to him and lay her arm across his chest.

"Menashe," she whispered. "I've not been with a man since Evin Prison ... I had never been with one before that either. I've never experienced the touch of a kind man, a man who was not an animal, and I vowed I never would. But it felt good to be in your arms last night, and it surprised me. We might well not live beyond tomorrow, and just once before I die I would like to feel what love is like. I know that after what I told you, you must think me unclean. I only wish ...."

He cradled her head on his shoulder, feeling himself stiffen. "Seriyah, you are the most remarkable woman I've ever met, and I could never think ill of you. I think you're brave and wonderful ... and beautiful." He drew her face close and kissed her gently on the lips and then on her neck, inhaling the aroma of her hair.

She responded, pressing herself against him. She sat up and began removing her clothes as Michael did the same, and then their bodies were pressed together again. She sighed softly as he entered her and stared at his face reflected in the light of the fire. Then she closed her eyes and arched her body into his. He made love to her slowly, gently, and when at last she came it was with a gentle shudder.

Afterwards, they lay close together enjoying the warmth of their embrace. They said nothing for a long while before she kissed him on the cheek and rose to put her clothes back on. He did the same. For the first time in weeks he slept soundly.

CHAPTER 28

"Wake up, my friend." Michael awoke with Karzan shaking his shoulder. "It will be dawn soon, and we must be on our way."

After a hearty breakfast Dimen gave each of them a hug, and they bundled into the Landcruiser, which proved to be much more comfortable than the truck with the bonus that the heater worked. Over her heavy clothing, Seriyah wore a black *chador* that Dimen's wife had provided. It covered her from head to toe and concealed part of her face. She and Michael would again play the roles of husband and wife as shown in their false identity documents.

The dark clouds of the night before had laid a new layer of snow over the fields, but the main roads were being cleared, and they were soon on a macadammed highway that carried them around the northern edge of Bijar before turning west. The new snow contributed to the lack of traffic around the city, and Karzan assured them that for at least the first half of the day's journey they should encounter few fellow travelers. Farther west, toward the border, the country was more settled. Marivan was a large city with well over 100,000 inhabitants. But the villages they were passing now were made up of low, single story mud buildings, and the land was mostly agricultural, much of it, Michael knew, dedicated to growing poppies.

Farther west of Bijar there was no new snow, and the highway was completely clear, allowing them to pick up speed.

"You should see it in the summer," said Karzan. "It's really beautiful. And one day we'll drive the fucking Iranians out."

"I wish you luck," said Michael, "but right now I just want to get it all behind me."

"We'll get you out. All we must do is get past the border guards. There is a major outpost near Marivan with a lot of troops."

About eighty kilometers outside Marivan traffic on the road picked up as they entered a more developed area. Karzan produced a military grade walkie-talkie that Michael had not seen before. In response to his curious glance, Karzan said, "I need to contact some friends. You didn't think I was going to get you across the border all by myself, did you?"

He began calling out on the walkie-talkie, pressing the send button and speaking at ten-minute intervals until finally there was a faint, scratchy response. After another few kilometers, the signal was clear, and Karzan began speaking in rapid Kurdish, which Michael could barely understand.

His conversation finished, Karzan said, "Apparently, the border is alive with Iranian troops. They're expecting a crossing attempt." His tone did not imply that he was especially concerned.

"Is there a plan?" asked Michael.

"There is always a plan, my friend. We'll find out what it is when we join my men." He checked the rear-view mirror, smiled, and said, "Ah, here they are now."

Michael swiveled his head and saw a Land Rover of indeterminate age and a Nissan pick-up truck approaching rapidly from behind. The Land Rover passed them sounding a blast on its horn, and Karzan waved at the bearded face of the man in the passenger seat.

"Isn't it a little dangerous to form up in a convoy like this?" asked Michael.

"We're in my country now," said Karzan. "No one will bother us, but if they do, they'll regret it."

They followed the Land Rover for several kilometers before turning off the main road onto a rutted dirt track that led through an olive grove, the gnarled trunks and branches of the ancient trees black and stark against the gray, winter sky.

Moments later they arrived at a farmhouse, another low, mud structure surrounded by a wall. There were five men in the other two cars. They each greeted Karzan with an embrace and a kiss, a sign of respect. Everyone entered the farmhouse where the men stared curiously at Michael and Seriyah.

Given the increased border patrol presence in the mountains, making it to the border presented a challenge. To improve their chances, Karzan's men would ambush a patrol, creating a diversion that would draw troops to the site, hopefully leaving a gap through which they could pass undetected.

It would be tough going in the snow, and they would leave tracks, which was not good, but no one was going to send in a helicopter to pick them up and drop them into Kurdistan. Michael felt a sense of infinite gratitude to these Kurds who would risk all for him and Seriyah. Yes, they would be compensated with weapons and money, but what was that when measured against one's life? The dangerous operation would achieve no Kurdish goal; its sole purpose was to provide them safe passage.

But safe passage did not mean easy passage. It was still winter, and the mountains were covered with snow that was waist deep in some areas. These were the Zagros Mountains that lay between Iran and Iraq. Mirabad sat on the shores of Lake Zeribar, a huge body of water north and west of the city. Karzan's route took them south of the lake and into the mountains where they would begin the hardest part of the journey.

Just after sunset they set off on foot from the Land Rover, which one of Karzan's men drove away, presumably eventually to return it to its owner in Bijar. The clouds of earlier in the day had given way to a clear sky, and the countryside was silvered by moonlight which both aided them and put them in greater danger.

They hid in the shadow of a deep ravine, waiting for the ambush to get underway. It was set up south of a near-by village on a road that paralleled the border over which the patrols regularly passed. The sudden, clattering din of guns and exploding RPG's reached them, and Michael recognized the deep throated roar of a 50-caliber machinegun.

"Time to go," announced Karzan. He looped a long rope around each of their waists. "Footing will be treacherous. We'll try to stick to the ridgelines because the snow is very deep at the bottom of the ravines."

"How far to the border?" asked Michael.

"Only a few more kilometers as the crow flies," said Karzan, "but the path we'll follow is not direct. It's going to take us a while."

"Do your friends on the other side of the border know we're coming?"

"Oh, yes. And we'll be in radio contact as soon as we clear a few ridgelines."

Karzan led the way. Seriyah was in the middle, and Michael brought up the rear. The two men carried Kalashnikovs slung over their shoulders, and Karzan had given the submachinegun to Seriyah. "You should have it," he'd said. "You earned it."

Their eyes adjusted quickly to the moonlight, and showed the terrain was as rugged as promised, but Karzan was intimately familiar with the route. He had passed over it many times and led them unhesitatingly forward. They were slowed slightly by Seriyah, who could not match the men's stride.

The sound of gunfire from the ambush reverberated through the mountains as they advanced. Suddenly Karzan raised a hand to halt them and cocked his head, listening. Michael heard it, as well – the staccato thump of helicopter blades. The sound was behind them and heading in the direction of the battle. Looking back, they could see the running lights as it headed south.

"Shit," said Karzan. "My men won't be able to hold out much longer if that chopper attacks them with rockets. We need to move faster." He looked at Seriyah. "Can you do it?"

"Yes," she replied. "I'll do my best."

Karzan picked up the pace, but it was tough going, the snow in places reaching their knees. From behind they heard the thump of rockets striking targets, and Michael hoped Karzan's men could escape the mayhem.

"They will fade into the countryside," said Karzan, "but the Iranians will pursue them. They may still buy us time. We must move farther to the north before turning west to the border."

The sounds of battle faded to silence as Karzan at last veered west. "The border is only a few kilometers ahead now," he said.

Seriyah was gasping for breath, and Michael said, "Karzan. We have to rest for a moment. Seriyah's about had it."

The big Kurd didn't like it. "We need to hurry. These last few kilometers we'll be in the open, and on a clear night like this we could be spotted."

As if on cue, the sound of an approaching helicopter came from behind them.

"They might have figured out that the ambush was a ruse," said Karzan, "and are now sweeping the border area. We have to move, now!"

"I'll be all right," gasped Seriyah as she struggled to her feet. Let's go."

Karzan set a faster pace through the snow, which was not so deep on this side of the mountains but from behind the helicopter came ever nearer like an angry hornet as it swept a bright searchlight in a zigzag pattern over the ground.

"Get down," Karzan shouted, "and don't move or they'll spot us for sure."

But the chopper was on them in a minute, and they were caught in the bright circle of the searchlight. The craft was low to the ground as it swooped past and made an abrupt one hundred eighty degree turn back toward them before it was more than a hundred meters past. Machinegun fire erupted from its nose and impacted all around them, kicking up snow, dirt, and shards of rock.

Karzan spoke quickly into the walkie-talkie as the chopper turned to make another pass at them and a series of eruptions threw snow high in the air as the machine gun rounds impacted in straight, parallel lines heading directly toward them. Michael held the girl tight, covering her body with his as he waited for the bullets to reach them.

A constellation of tracer rounds tore skyward from the other side of the border as a heavy machinegun chattered.

"Move!" shouted Karzan.

They sprang to their feet and began to run, their bodies charged with adrenaline, in the direction of the gunfire. The Iranian helicopter surged toward them again, but there was the whoosh of a rocket above them as someone fired an RPG at it. The rocket missed, but it and the barrage of machinegun fire discouraged the helicopter crew, and they turned to run for safety.

Minutes later, they ran into the arms of a group of armed men who already were disassembling the machinegun and loading it into the back of a pick-up truck.

They untied the rope from around their waists, and Michael and Seriyah collapsed to the ground as Karzan was embraced by some of the men.

One of the burly armed men dressed in military fatigues approached them, and Michael was surprised to hear a familiar voice address him in Hebrew, "*Mizman loh hitraehnu, Michael.* Long time no see, Michael. What took you so long?"

"Ronan?" Despite his fatigue Michael leapt to his feet. It was hard to believe his eyes. "What the hell are you doing here?"

"I needed some fresh, mountain air and thought this was as good a place as any." He embraced Michael in a bearhug that squeezed what little breath he had left out of him. Then he stepped back and rested his hands over Michael's shoulders, and his voice became serious. "We feared we had lost you, Michael."

"I would have been lost – several times – were it not for our friends."

Ronan seemed to notice Seriyah for the first time. She was still sitting, catching her breath.

"And who is this?" asked Ronan.

"Someone who saved my life. We're going to take her with us."

Ronan blinked, surprised. "That's not part of the plan."

"I don't care, Eitan, she's coming with us."

"She?" Dressed as she was, Ronan had taken Seriyah for a boy."

She got to her feet. Looking at Michael, she said, "I don't understand a word of what you're saying. Who is this man, Menashe?"

Ronan did not understand the Farsi, but his eyes widened when he heard the girl say Michael's true name.

Michael shifted to English. "Seriyah, this is

Eitan, my boss. Eitan, this is Seriyah who saved my life more than once." He looked hard into Ronan's eyes. "She's coming with us back to Israel."

Before Ronan could speak, Seriyah said, "Don't I have something to say about this? I don't want to go anywhere, least of all a country where I would be considered an enemy. I want to stay here and fight."

Karzan was attracted by their conversation and joined the group. He and Ronan were strikingly similar, substantial and powerful, warriors for their respective causes. To Ronan he said, "I understand you've come a long way to be here. I hope you're satisfied with our services."

Ronan studied the Kurd. "You must be the famous Karzan these men have been talking about. And, yes, we are most satisfied and grateful for what you have done, and that gratitude will be expressed in material form very soon."

Karzan grunted his satisfaction and started to walk away, but Seriyah grabbed him by the sleeve. "Karzan, I want to stay here with you. I want to fight."

The Kurd eyed her speculatively, "Well, I know you can fight, and you're tougher than you look, but you're not a Kurd. We can talk about it later. Right now, I just want to go home."

Everyone bundled into the pick-up truck and a Nissan SUV. Some time later they passed through the streets of a village east of Erbil. Karzan, Ronan, Michael, and Seriyah were dropped off in front of a large, well-built house on the outskirts of the village. "Welcome to my home," said Karzan. "You will be safe here tonight while arrangements are made for your departure."

The interior of the house was impressive, richly

furnished and boasting many precious carpets. Michael recognized the patterns as the same as those he had seen at Karzan's cousin's house in Bijar.

They were greeted by an attractive woman whom Michael took to be Karzan's wife and two young children, a boy and a girl, who wrapped their arms around the fierce Kurd. Karzan smiled broadly and lifted both children in his arms to smother them with kisses.

Turning to Michael and Seriyah, his children now pulling his beard, Karzan said, "Things are much better here now, thanks the Brits and the Americans who protect us from that bastard Saddam. No more poison gas, no more bombing. We have the possibility of building a strong, independent Kurdish state. But enough of politics. You are exhausted. My wife will show you to your rooms. You can take a hot shower and change into more comfortable clothing."

The hot shower felt like the closest thing to heaven Michael had ever experienced. His cold skin tingled as the hot water flowed over him, and he just stood there under the stream feeling his muscles relax. Afterwards, he found clothing laid out for him in the bedroom, a pair of tan slacks and a turtleneck sweater, and sturdy, but comfortable shoes. For a moment he wondered how they had known his size and then realized Ronan must have brought the clothes with him.

Seriyah's determination to remain with Karzan worried him. She could find a new home in Israel in the large Iranian community there. Yes, as a Shiite Muslim she would be an anomaly, but he was certain his family would be happy to take her in. She did not seem to be particularly religious, and quite likely was not, given her experience with religious fanatics. For that matter, most Israelis were not particularly religious either. He resolved to convince her to leave with them, and he didn't care what Ronan might have to say about it.

But he had to talk to her first.

Karzan's home was spacious and quite modern, unlike the mud brick construction to which Michael had become accustomed. Erbil, of course, was a large city of nearly a million people and one of the oldest inhabited spaces on the planet. Karzan was obviously a wealthy man, and whether his wealth came from trading, smuggling, or robbery Michael did not care.

When he returned to the living room, he found that his host also had changed clothing. In gabardine slacks and a V-neck sweater over a starched white shirt, he had also trimmed his beard and looked every inch the prosperous merchant. He and Ronan were bent toward one another deep in conversation.

"Am I interrupting something important?" asked Michael.

"Come join us," said Ronan. "We're discussing how you and I are getting out of here and back home."

"Don't forget Seriyah."

Ronan sighed. "We're not forgetting her. She stated quite clearly that she intends to remain."

"We can use her in the Peshmerga," added Karzan. "She is brave and more than proved herself."

"Yes," said Michael, "she's brave, but she deserves a little peace, some time apart from life and death situations. She's more fragile than you might think."

"Are you talking about me again?" Seriyah's voice sounded from behind him.

"Yes," said Michael, turning toward her. She was again as he had first seen her, in blue jeans and a dark sweater, her hair down around her shoulders. "Karzan, Ronan, will you allow me to speak to her alone?"

"Of course," said Karzan. He pointed to a doorway. "You may use the dining room."

When they were alone, Michael said, "Seriyah, you don't have to stay here. I want you to come with me. You can be safe and happy."

"I don't think I can ever be happy," she said. "That option may be closed to me."

"You don't know that. You need to give yourself a chance, at least."

"Your country is the enemy of my country. I could never be accepted."

"You're wrong, and what's worse you're repeating the propaganda of the mullahs. Why should you think they're lying about everything else but telling the truth about Israel?"

She lowered her gaze. "You're right, of course. Nothing they say is to be trusted. But still, my place is here doing whatever I can against them."

"You can't go back to Iran," he said, "and you're a foreigner, a citizen of a nation with which the Kurds are at war."

"The Kurds are Shiites like me ..."

"But you're not a Kurd, either. Seriyah, I want you to come with us. I want you, not a country."

His words surprised even him. He'd not realized how deeply he'd come to care for this strange Iranian girl with whom he had absolutely nothing in common. Some switch had been thrown inside him releasing a current that connected him to her, like the attraction between opposite poles of a magnet.

She looked at him with wide, troubled eyes. "Menashe," she said, "what happened between us the other night was an impulse, something unexpected, most of all by me. I don't know what I think, what I feel. It's all muddled and chaotic. So much has happened. When Farhood and I agreed to help you, we thought it would be romantic and exciting. We didn't think of the consequences. It was a chance for us to really do something, at last. But it wasn't like that. It was terrible and tragic, and so much blood has been spilled. Farhood is lost forever. I can't help but believe I owe him something."

He took her hand. "Seriyah, you owe it to him to be safe and happy. Live your life and find some sort of fulfillment. Don't you think that's what he would want more than anything? I promise you it's possible. I won't abandon you. You won't be alone."

"You would stay with me, Menashe?"

"I think I want to marry you, Seriyah. What do you say?"

Tears welled in her eyes, and she buried her face in his shoulder. "Menashe ..."

YEKATERINBURG

The train traversed Sverdlovsk Oblast where Europe ends and Asia begins in the southern district city of Magnitogorsk. The ancient mountains here are low, gentle slopes, rounded by the centuries and covered with forest. Mighty rivers flow north to spill into the Arctic Ocean. It was so unlike tiny Israel that it might as well have been another planet.

CHAPTER 29

Tel Aviv

"I want you to go to Vienna and link up with Sasha."

Ronan was back in the *memuneh's* office. They had just finished debriefing Michael Mossberg on the Iranian operation.

"First things first, David," said Ronan. "What about Michael and this Iranian girl?"

"The man wants to marry her. What can I say?"

"You could say no."

"And then we would lose one of our best operatives, and you would have to train a new *Kidon* member. Who knows how it will work out. It's odd, of course, an Israeli marrying an Iranian Muslim, but in the end they're both Iranian. Maybe it will work out."

"He can't take her back to Switzerland, and the job is not finished there with the Russians."

"Give them some time. Michael said his new wife

could settle with his family in Ashdod after the honeymoon. He can return to Switzerland then to finish the job. And we might have something on the horizon that will speed that along. It's why I need your team in Vienna."

"What is it?"

"Our friend in Paris has alerted us to an interesting American operation there. The man is clever. He set it up for the American operative to contact Sasha for support. He will have no idea she is Mossad, of course."

"So, what's it about?"

"Apparently, there's a KGB bookkeeper on the loose there, and the Americans have an interest in him."

"Sounds like a longshot. I'm not crazy about the Americans."

"I know, but the poor bastards occasionally need some help, to be prodded in the right direction. I'm hoping you and Sasha can do that without raising too much dust. But try to be efficient. I need Sasha for another job."

Ronan raised his eyebrows.

"I want her to go to Russia, to Sverdlovsk, to be exact."

"You want her to re-contact the KGB officer who gave us the Iran operation." It was a statement, not a question.

"Precisely, but since they split up the KGB, we don't know if he's SVR or FSB. I only hope he's still in Sverdlovsk. Our enemies have been recruiting Russian scientists by the dozen. It poses a serious problem, and maybe a tame Russian intelligence officer can help."

Sasha Turmarkina stared out the train window and contemplated the vastness of Russia. Her journey required twenty-four hours and entering a different time zone to reach Yekaterinburg from Moscow. But she trusted Russian trains more than Russian planes. Much had happened in the last few months that gave her a great deal to think about. The operation in Vienna had turned unexpectedly violent and brought her together with a resourceful American with whom a relationship had developed that frightened and attracted her in equal measure. She welcomed the assignment to Russia as an opportunity to clear her head.

The train traversed Sverdlovsk Oblast where Europe ends and Asia begins in the southern district city of Magnitogorsk. The ancient mountains here are low, gentle slopes, rounded by the centuries and covered with forest. Mighty rivers flow north to spill into the Arctic Ocean. It was so unlike tiny Israel that it might as well have been another planet.

Summer was nearing its end and temperatures were dropping, but it was still comfortably warm during the day. The train arrived at the main station in the center of Yekaterinburg. Sasha was traveling light, with only one bag. She didn't plan to stay for long – just long enough to find Nikolay Kozlov – if he were still assigned to Yekaterinburg.

She'd reserved a room at a tourist hotel not far from the station. After the dissolution of the Soviet Union, Russia had opened up, and she was traveling as an Austrian tourist. But she would take no chances that Russian vigilance against espionage had been relaxed as much as travel controls.

The hotel was within walking distance, according to the city map she bought at the train station, so she set off on foot, checking for surveillance. She saw none. It was late in the afternoon, and she decided to call it a day and get to business in the morning.

The contact plan was simple. In fact, there was no contact plan because Kozlov had wanted no part of it in Vienna. So, she fell back to basics and would call him at his office and set up a meeting. It wasn't the best of plans, but she knew nothing of Kozlov's habits, so arranging a "chance meeting" was off the table.

She ate a very mediocre breakfast at the hotel next morning and read the local papers until nine a.m. Kozlov would surely be in his office by this hour. She set off on foot and wandered aimlessly for an hour. Reassured that she was not under surveillance, she found a pay phone and called the number Ronan had given her for Kozlov's office.

A woman answered. "Regional FSB. State your business."

Breaking up the old KGB wrought many changes, and one of them was that some employees found themselves in the SVR (actually the old First Chief Directorate) and others ended up in the FSB, which assumed internal security responsibilities. It made sense that the local office had been remanded to the FSB.

"May I speak to Nikolay Kozlov, please?" she asked.

"What is your business with Major Kozlov?"

"It's a family matter. I'm his cousin visiting Yekaterinburg for a few days."

After an uncomfortable pause, the call was passed through to Kozlov's office.

"Who is calling, please?" he asked.

"It's your cousin, Svetlana, from Moscow," she said.

"Svetlana ....?"

Before he could say more, she hurried on. "I'm your Uncle Ronan's daughter," she said. "He very much wanted me to meet you while I'm here."

Kozlov caught on fast. "When and where?"

She'd found a café during the morning's walk. It was suitably off the beaten track and from a concealment across the street she could watch Kozlov arrive and enter the café.

She gave him the coordinates and set the meeting for six p.m.

The next several hours were spent wandering around the city. Fortunately, it was a nice day, somewhat warmer than expected. She found the parklands along the river very attractive and sat there on a bench watching the ducks for a long time. She found a small restaurant for lunch. The old churches offered refuge where she could sit for long periods without attracting notice. She didn't want to go back to the hotel in case anyone had decided to surveil her.

She was tired after a day on her feet, moving from one place to another by the time the sun was on the horizon and the hour for the meeting approached. Across the street from the café she waited, hoping enough daylight remained for her to identify Kozlov from the photo Ronan had provided so she could memorize the man's face.

He was not hard to recognize. He was dressed in mufti, a suit much too well-cut to be of Soviet manufacture. She recalled that he had been stationed in Paris where he must have acquired the suit. Kozlov had movie star good looks with blondish hair and a thin moustache. He stamped out a cigarette, and before entering the café surveyed the area, his eyes zeroing in on Sasha's hiding place. She was certain he could not see her, but he had easily identified the best counter-surveillance site in the area. The guy was sharp.

She waited another ten minutes but saw nothing to arouse suspicion. Finally, still checking her peripheral vision, she crossed the street and entered the café.

Kozlov had selected a table in the rear and sat facing the door. His eyes followed her as she crossed the room and sat at his side, where she also could keep an eye on the entrance. He'd ordered tea, and two cups sat on the table.

He lit another cigarette and studied her through the smoke. "My dear cousin," he said with a twitch of his lips. "I had no idea that Uncle Ronan had such a lovely daughter. Please, sit down. Your tea is getting cold."

Sasha was accustomed to men looking at her. She appeared several years younger than her actual age, and she had emphasized that today by wearing jeans, knee boots, a light sweater and a jacket.

"Thank you for meeting me," she said. "Uncle Ronan has a few questions he'd like answered."

"And so, he sends a girl into the lion's den to get the answers? A little dangerous, don't you think?"

"Not really," she said, staring him down. "Don't be fooled by what you see."

He returned her stare and gave her a tight smile. "I quite like what I see. It's what you want that worries me. I told my 'uncle' that I had no interest in further contact. I told him what I thought he should know, and that was it. I know what happened to Vinogradov in Paris, by the way, and I'm not sure how I feel about it."

"Things did not go exactly according to plan in Paris," she said. "We did what we had to do."

His eyes widened in surprise. "You were there?"

"That's not important," she replied. "What is important is what we have to talk about now."

"We'll see," he said as he placed his elbows on the table and leaned toward her. "What do you want to know?"

"Have you told anyone you are meeting me?"

"Of course not."

"Good. It would end badly for both of us."

His eyes clouded at the implied threat, and she instantly regretted being too aggressive. "I'm sorry," she said. "It's a touchy situation, and I have no desire to remain here any longer than necessary."

"Go on," he said cautiously.

"We are hearing about other Soviet CBW scientists and technicians being recruited by questionable people like the Iranians, Syrians, and Iraqis. Can you tell me what you know about this? We also would like the names and specialties of the people involved."

He chewed this over for several beats before answering. "I can see why you're concerned. There is a lot going on with our scientific community these days, and it's not such a big secret. In fact, our government and the Americans are working together to prevent what could be a dangerous brain drain. Programs are being set up to provide alternate employment, and there is a lot of money being offered. The main concern is for nuclear scientists, especially those who worked in the defense industry."

"And what about the CBW types?"

"Ah, that is another matter entirely. Have you ever heard of *Biopreparat*?"

"No. What about it?"

Kozlov shook his head sadly. "In the early 1970's we signed an international agreement to cease all production of CB weapons. Of course, the Soviet Union did not comply. An organization called *Biopreparat* became responsible for all biotechnological production in the country. On the surface it is responsible for the development of pharmaceuticals and vaccines, but that is only a cover. Along with the Ministry of Defense it runs dozens of secret research facilities, including one here in Yekaterinburg, to support a biochemical warfare capability. Tens of thousands work in these facilities, including scientists, and they all know their work is in direct contravention of international law. Today, Moscow is in no position to admit to the Americans what *Biopreparat* really does, and so the CBW scientists and technicians aren't receiving the new training or alternative jobs and stipends like the workers in the nuclear industry. The organization is being downsized now, and that means there are a lot of people with some very dangerous knowledge looking for a way to survive."

Sasha was aghast at the scope of what Kozlov had said. Thousands of potential recruits for the enemies of Israel! "Well," she said, "that's a terrifying vision."

"It gets worse," said Kozlov. "The situation in Russia today is like the Wild West. Nearly anything goes. Some senior military officers are even selling weapons out of storage bunkers. Russia has become an open buffet for illegal weapons sales, narcotics, money laundering. Anything goes these days. And it will only get worse until someday another strongman comes along and takes over the government. Of course, that is inevitable. It is Russia, after all."

"Is there any way to find out which scientists have been recruited out of the country and where they have gone, what their specialties are?"

He nodded. "Yes. The FSB tries to keep track but is not always successful. And there's something else, for all the good it will do to tell you."

She waited for him to continue.

He shook his head again. "There is a group, a sort of secret society of former KGB officers, some still serving in the FSB or SVR. Rumor has it that the group's leader is General Yuriy Ivanovich Morozov, quite a famous and powerful man. Right now, they're biding their time, discovering ways to accumulate wealth and power, but some day when Russia is nearly on her knees, they will take over the country. And the sad fact is that the people will welcome them. They'll welcome stability, no matter how it is achieved or the human cost."

"There's nothing we can do about that," said Sasha.

"No," he replied. "And there's nothing I can do either. I'm going to stay out here, far away from Moscow and its mechanizations. I'm going to keep my head down, just like everyone else."

"That's sad," she said.

He lit another cigarette and nodded wearily. "Yes, it's all very *grustno*, sad. But that's Russia. What the people really want is another Tsar, complete with an *Oprichina* to keep everyone in line. We Russians like to be told what to do, what to believe in, how to think. We don't like to think for ourselves. Better to let the Kremlin handle it."

The meeting was turning out to be unexpectedly non-productive. Perhaps she could salvage something. "You said there is a list of the scientists who have left the country?"

"I said we try to keep track of them."

"So, that means there's a list."

He took a long drag on his cigarette, tilted his head back and blew smoke into the air. "There is a list," he said at last.

"Can you get it for me?"

Red Page[16]

---

[16] Red Page" is the Mossad's code name for an order to kill someone. Each of these orders is jointly authorized by the Israeli prime minister and defense minister. "Red Pages" do not have to be executed right away. In fact, they have no expiration date, and the orders remain valid until they are expressly cancelled. Der Spiegel Online, 19 January 2010.

Michael had a premonition of misfortune. Seville was a bad luck city for Jews, after all. It is a city of sparkling history. But it also was the venue for the first auto da fe of the Spanish Inquisition and the beginning of the persecution of Jews in Spain. In 1492 Jews were expelled from the country to join the diaspora in exile.

CHAPTER 30

Khalid Barghouti the Palestinian was not impressed, but he had to pretend he was. The man before him was no longer the handsome young colonel and revolutionary of twenty years ago. In place of the careful grooming was a head of long, tightly curled hair that stood out from the head like a fright wig. The dark face had developed more lines, and the unfocused eyes and somnolent demeanor suggested drug use. The man was dressed outlandishly, in Barghouti's opinion, in a flowing crimson robe covered with strange designs and a matching brimless cloth cap on his head. The manner was arrogant, like that of an ancient Eastern potentate.

It was the first time Barghouti had seen Muammar Gaddafi in the flesh, the "Brotherly Leader and Guide of the Revolution of Libya." The man had been born in a tent to Bedouin parents who were goat and camel herders. It was said that he still was most comfortable in the desert. Perhaps that was why this audience was taking place in an air-conditioned tent in the Libyan desert well south of Tripoli.

Barghouti was amazed to discover that Gaddafi's personal body guard was truly made up entirely of attractive women, Amazons, all dressed in well-tailored military uniforms and posted at regular intervals around the tent, inside and out. He'd thought it was a myth.

The Palestinian was not the only visitor. To his left was an Iraqi, and to his right stood a Nigerian. All of them were supplicants who had come hat in hand to the Libyan dictator in search of funding. The light, sweet crude that flowed like milk from Libya's soil allowed Gaddafi to spread benevolence to numerous terrorist groups, and there was a regular stream of visitors seeking his favor. They usually walked away with a few million dollars that meant little to Gaddafi but made him an object of adulation among the more efficient bombers and murderers of the world. It gave him influence and power well beyond the frontiers of his country and elevated his opinion of himself beyond reasonable bounds.

Khalid Barghouti from Gaza was a relative newcomer to the terrorist trade. Strangely enough, he was a pediatrician, trained at Egypt's Zagazig University where he had fallen under the influence of the Muslim Brotherhood and learned the finer elements of the Islamist art of hate.

Using the clandestine organizational tactics he'd learned from the Brotherhood, Barghouti now headed the Palestinian Jihadist Army, the PJA.

These days he lived in Damascus where he had developed relations with the Iranians, who thought it a good idea to fund his murderous activities. He also had support from the United States where one of his deputies was a professor at the University of South Florida in Tampa and managed Palestinian "charitable" organizations that collected cash and found ways to get it to Barghouti's organization.

On this occasion, though Gaddafi's money would be a welcome contribution to the cause, but what Barghouti wanted even more was alias documentation as a Libyan which would permit him to travel more freely. Within the month there was a meeting he must attend. If all went well he would soon possess a weapon that promised to devastate the Israeli enemy.

CHAPTER 31

Tel Aviv, May 1995

Michael Mossberg descended from the taxi and surveyed the guarded gates of the anonymous building that served as Mossad Headquarters. Since the end of his assignment in Switzerland, he had worked in a satellite building in downtown Tel Aviv. The summons to meet with David Shalev, the *memuneh*, had come the day before, and he was intrigued.

He had settled into family life surprisingly comfortably. After some initial hesitation, Seriyah Esfahani had accepted his proposal, and now, after nearly two years of marriage, they had a fine son they had named Farhood and lived in an apartment in Tel Aviv not far from the sea.

Shalev remained seated behind his desk when Michael entered the office. The *memuneh* wore an ageless brown tweed suit that looked a size too large. The man was shrinking, as though he were being slowly eaten away by the burdens of his position. The deep lines on a face already shrunken with age and the bags under his eyes were testaments to too many sleepless nights. And these had been numerous in the wake of a wave of new terrorist depredations.

A year earlier, Hamas had initiated a series of ghastly bombings, the first coinciding with Holocaust Memorial Day when a young Palestinian drove a car loaded with gas cylinders, explosives, and rusty nails into a crowd of students, killing eight and wounding over 100. More atrocities followed. In October 1994 the most horrific attack took place in the center of Tel Aviv when a Palestinian wearing a suicide vest detonated next to a bus, strewing body parts in all directions. Twenty-two people were killed. Hamas jubilantly declared its responsibility.

Early 1995 saw the beginning of an even worse series of bombings. But this time it was not Hamas. There was a new organization unaffiliated with the known terrorist groups. It called itself the Palestinian Jihadist Army. If anything, the PJA was more radical even than Hamas, with no goals beyond the creation of chaos and death in Israel.

"Sit down, Michael." Shalev gestured at one of the chairs in front of his desk. "It's good to see you. I hear that things with you and your lovely wife are going well. Congratulations on the birth of your son."

Shalev had sent a small, silver *Bar Mitzvah* cup as a gift when Farhood was born. Michael was unsure whether it ever would be used. He planned to leave the choice of religion up to his son, but the cup was no less appreciated. "Thank you for the gift, David," he said. "It was very thoughtful of you. Seriyah sends her best."

Shalev smiled thinly and steepled his fingers. His gray eyes, magnified by thick glasses, demanded all of Michael's attention. The pleasantries out of the way, he wanted to get down to business. "I'm reactivating your

Kidon status. We've had a bit of luck, and I see an opportunity for decisive action. I've chosen you for three reasons: first, your work in Switzerland gave you an intimate familiarity with how the Russians operate; second, you understand how money works; and third, you know Spain very well.

"We have come to understand how terrorist-related organizations, such as the PLO, Hamas, and Hezbollah are funded. Without the illicit funds that flow into their accounts from all over the world, the terrorists could not purchase weapons or pay off the families of their "martyrs." Islamic "charities" in the United States and Lebanese Shiite communities in Latin America funnel enormous sums to support anti-Israeli violence. Much of the money pours also into the coffers of Iran's Quds force and from there to Hezbollah. One of our primary goals is to expose and cripple these funding sources.

"Are you familiar with the work of COGAT?[17]"

"Yes. It's part of the military, isn't it?"

"That's right, and the people who work in COGAT are, shall we say, familiar with intelligence work. These people speak fluent, Palestinian accented Arabic and know all the players in the Territories. The information they collect is irreplaceable and has permitted us to forestall many acts of terror. We've just received a bit of intelligence we can't ignore, something that demands

---

[17] COGAT – "COGAT is responsible for implementing the civilian policy within Judea and Samaria and towards the Gaza Strip, in coordination and cooperation with officials from defense and government offices in various fields. The unit is subordinate to Israel's Minister of Defense and to the Major General of the unit, who is a member of the General Staff of the IDF." http://www.cogat.mod.gov.il/en/about/Pages/default.aspx

immediate action to prevent what can only be termed a catastrophe. The Office has been given this assignment. It will be your responsibility."

Michael said nothing, knowing that Shalev now would go into the details. The *Kidon* reactivation was not entirely unwelcome, but whether he should share the information with Seriyah was another question. They had settled into a comfortable life in Tel Aviv, but he missed field work. Seriyah had been granted Israeli citizenship, but she was still a wanted person in Iran, and it would be dangerous for her to travel outside the country which precluded a long foreign assignment. She had not been without him since his return from Switzerland, and the Mossad had been most understanding. He was worried about how she would react to the news that he would be away.

Shalev continued. "COGAT has learned that the head of the PJA, Khalid Barghouti, is in Libya, and one of our agents in Damascus confirms it. What is more, Barghouti plans to travel to Spain for a meeting with an influential Russian. The meeting was arranged by Iranian intelligence, and an Iranian representative might well also attend the meeting. The Iranians have thus far been a major source of funding for the PJA, and now have big plans for it."

"How are the Russians involved?" asked Michael.

"Ah, that is the key." Shalev removed his glasses and rubbed his eyes. "The Russians will never change, it seems. They like to meddle for meddling's sake just to stir up trouble, to keep the pot boiling. For some insane reason, they think it helps them. We learned a few years ago just how the remnants of the old KGB are working to regain total control in Russia and how closely they have become aligned with the so-called Russian Mafia. They scratch one another's backs in many ways. We broke up their operations in Spain and Zürich, as you know.

"Now they're at it again, this time intending to do terrible damage to our country and fill their coffers while doing it. To answer your question, the Russians are involved because they are prepared to provide chemical warfare agents to the PJA, for a price, of course. That's where the Iranians come in. They provide the money, the Russians provide the means, and the PJA is the delivery system."

Michael was horrified. "That sounds terribly irresponsible, even for the Russians. What kind of chemical agent?"

"I agree, and we don't fully understand how the Russians could take such a risk. They must know we would track the chemical agent back to them. We're not sure what the chemical is. It could be sarin or something newer and even more deadly. We know that the Iranians already produce sarin, so it's probably the latter. The Russians never entirely shut down their research. The KGB and its predecessors have maintained a secret poison laboratory since the 1920's, and the SVR has kept them going. But we're not sure where this batch is coming from. It could well originate in weapons storage facilities. Russian officers have been selling all kinds of equipment on the black market."

Michael's body went cold. A chemical attack on Israel would be devastating. "Do we know the identity of the Russian?"

"Yes, thanks to our source in Russia. The FSB recently arrested an Army colonel suspected of illegally selling expensive military equipment out of the armory he managed. Under interrogation he admitted selling the chemical weapons to a mafioso named Sergei Gromov who lives near Seville, where he also owns a luxury hotel. I would suspect the hotel is the most likely venue for a meeting. Gromov is a former KGB officer and a wily sort. He made a lot of money working with the Chechen mafia in the early days, and for that reason is not a favorite of his compatriots. He had no choice about leaving Russia."

"Maybe he's operating alone."

"Maybe. We have no way of knowing."

"What about Barghouti?"

All we know for the time being is that he will travel to Spain via a circuitous route before returning to Damascus, and the meeting is set for mid-May.

"Why not just eliminate Barghouti before he makes the meeting?"

"I agree it's a possibility, but we have to find him first. I'm not discarding the idea, but we would rather catch them all and leave a message that we will not tolerate such behavior, not from the Iranians and certainly not from the Russians."

"So, our best bet is to set up surveillance on Gromov?"

"For the time being, yes. Damascus is working on finding Barghouti, and our man at the El Al office in Madrid will watch flight manifests. It will take some luck because Barghouti undoubtedly will be traveling in alias. We do have photographs of him."

"It's a longshot. How many people will I have?"

"Will ten be enough for you?"

"At a minimum. You're talking about more than

one target, and surveillance requirements will be a strain."

"I know. But prudence dictates we keep it at a minimum. Be ready to leave tomorrow."

CHAPTER 32

Michael arrived home early and found Seriyah starting up the stairs to the apartment loaded down with string bags of groceries and Farhood in a baby carrier on her chest. She was surprised to see him and grateful when he unburdened her of the groceries. "Good timing," she smiled. "I'm exhausted."

She spoke in Hebrew, still with an accent she worked to overcome. But after two years she was comfortable with the language. She insisted they speak it at home and reverted to Farsi only when they visited Michael's family in Ashdod or when she scolded Michael. "If I'm going to live here," she'd said, "I may as well go entirely native."

He kissed her on the cheek and ran his hand over the down on Farhood's head, a father's pride welling in his chest. Unbidden came the thought that this would be the first time he'd been separated from his family since returning from Switzerland.

After an emotional farewell with Karzan, they'd boarded an unmarked Blackhawk helicopter crewed by amazingly incurious Americans who ferried them to an airfield outside Bagdad. An anonymous Lear Jet took them from there to Ben Gurion Airport in Tel Aviv. It had been a remarkably calm, well-ordered exfiltration, especially when compared with the untidy escape from Iran.

Seriyah stayed with his family in Ashdod while Michael completed his mission in Switzerland, which took only a little over a month.

Now, in this cozy apartment with a wife and son he loved, the thought that he might never see them again if things should go south in Spain sprang upon him like a Hamas ambush. He'd never much considered the consequences of putting himself at risk as a *Kidon* member. In effect, he'd been married to Israel, and he carried her always with him wherever he might be, the center of his life. Like Boadicea, Israel had been forced into war, and Michael had answered her call. She'd whispered in his ear about duty and cheered when he took risks and was successful. And he knew she would be with him if he met an unfortunate end.

But now his center of gravity had shifted to Seriyah and little Farhood. He could not escape the fear that he might now take fewer risks, might second guess what had to be done, and worst of all, doubt the possibility of success. Did he still possess what *Kidon* demanded at the tip of the spear? With an effort, he shoved such thoughts away. Indecision could lead to death, and he had every intention of returning to Israel.

The groceries put away and the baby now asleep in his crib, Seriyah asked, "Why are you home so early, and why do you suddenly look so grim?"

"I have to go away for a while," he said, "out of the country. I'll probably be gone for a couple of weeks. I leave tomorrow."

Her dark eyes seemed to swallow him, engulf his soul and penetrate to its core. "Will it be dangerous?"

she asked quietly.

"Maybe a little."

"Can you tell me about it? Are you going back to Iran?"

"No, not Iran, not anyplace with that sort of danger. But I can't tell you more."

She remained silent, staring at him, her eyes unreadable. "But only for a couple of weeks?"

"That should be all it takes," he replied. "While I'm away, I want you and Farhood to stay with my family in Ashdod."

"Why? We'll be alright here."

"I insist. These recent bombings make Tel Aviv unsafe, and my family wants to spend more time with the baby. Think of it as a restful vacation where grandma and granddad will take care of everything. They'll be overjoyed."

"Will the Office know where I am?"

"Of course. I'll make sure they do, and you can contact them whenever you want. You know the *memuneh* has a soft spot for you."

She frowned slightly. "Do you think so? He's a strange little man."

"He's a giant in his own way but worn down by his responsibilities. He'll look after any of your needs."

"Is this a *Kidon* mission?"

He hesitated, but she deserved to know at least a small part of the truth. "Yes."

"But not as dangerous as it was in Iran?"

"Certainly not."

He wasn't convinced she believed him.

CHAPTER 33

Spain's Kodachrome sunlight is, if anything, most brilliant in Andalusia. Even now on an afternoon in May, it was wise to walk on the shady side of the street to avoid the 35°C heat. On this particular day in Seville, if one looked closely, a figure might be discerned in the deep shadow of a café veranda opposite the Hotel Reina Sevillana. The figure had been there nearly an hour at a table against the wall.

Were it possible to see the man's eyes behind the sunglasses, it would be noted that his gaze seldom wavered from the main entrance of the hotel. His interest heightened when a middle-aged couple alit from a taxi, retrieved their luggage from the boot and trundled through the doors, their suitcases on rollers trailing behind. The couple, the man knew, were traveling on British passports that identified them as residents of the Cottswolds, just outside of London.

The man in the shadow checked his watch and tilted his chair back against the cool, stone wall. He could be taken for a tourist with his baseball cap, blue jeans, and sneakers.

Twenty minutes later, two men arrived at the hotel in a taxi. They were dressed casually in Bermuda shorts and carried tennis racquets.

Fifteen minutes later, Michael Mossberg's cellphone vibrated in his pocket. He lifted it to his ear, listened, murmured a few words and closed the connection.

He paid his tab and walked away from the café, satisfied that the surveillance team had arrived as scheduled and checked into the hotel where they expected the arrival of Khalid Barghouti. It was a significant advantage knowing where the primary target would be staying and meeting with his Russian and Iranian contacts. Staking out an airport or train station and hoping to spot him among hundreds of other passengers would have been problematic for several reasons.

They knew where the Russian lived. Even if they somehow missed spotting Khalid Barghouti's arrival, eventually the Russian would lead them to him. Marc LeBrun from Paris was assigned to watch the house.

The Iranian remained a mystery.

All the equipment the team needed had been sent to Madrid via diplomatic pouch and passed to Michael before he boarded the train at Atocha Station. He had visited each team member in Seville to distribute the equipment. Only he and the two burly boys carrying Irish passports were to be armed. Cars were rented, and communications equipment tested. By the second day on the ground in Seville, they were ready.

The team was scattered around the city in different hotels. All the names used for the operation were aliases, supported either by forged or quite real passports that either had been volunteered to Israeli authorities by immigrants or occasionally pilfered from a hotel room when there was a requirement for a passport matching a certain type. Secure communications were assured by encrypted devices disguised as cell phones. Contact with the Office was provided via a commo cut-out in Vienna.

Il'yas Shishani was suspicious. This was the third time he'd spotted the same car parked along the riverfront near the house. There were many residences along the street. Cars came and went regularly, and there were always tourists admiring the historic river. But Il'yas, one of Sergei Gromov's Chechen bodyguards, had learned never to be complacent. He walked past the car and managed a quick glance inside. A man sat behind the steering wheel, but what really caught Il'yas's attention was the camera with a powerful telephoto lens on the seat beside him.

Il'yas was well-trained, and what he was seeing suggested surveillance. He could be wrong, but his intuition was strong that someone was paying too much attention to his boss' residence.

Unlike most of his *nouveau riche* Russian counterparts, who loved their villas along the Mediterranean coast, Sergei Gromov preferred city living. He bought a huge house in the Triana district of Seville along the Guadalquivir riverfront. It was rumored that the wealthy Russian was interested in purchasing a professional soccer team.

Gromov was a pariah in his own country. He'd made his fortune dealing with the Chechen mob, and this made him unpopular with the intelligence services and criminal police. It had become unhealthy for him to remain in Moscow.

His years in the old KGB made Gromov a careful man, but his caution was often overcome by greed. He'd never dreamed that such riches could be his, and his appetite for money was never sated. He kept his hand in the game whenever a money-making opportunity presented itself, and the profit from his current endeavor would be impressive.

Thanks to his Chechen friends, he had contacts with Jihadists all over the Middle East and often served as a conduit for arms sales to them. But such sales were insignificant compared to what he now offered the PJA who had turned to Iran for financial support.

In return for his help, the Chechens supplied him with three proficient bodyguards who were quartered in his house. One of them accompanied him at all times.

The news that his house might be under surveillance was annoying. The Spanish authorities occasionally took some interest in him, and this was a bad time for it to happen again. With such a huge transaction in a few days and a crate of chemical weapons in his basement, any sign of trouble was alarming. He doubled his normal bodyguard.

The Palestinian and the Iranian would soon be in Seville. The Palestinian would relieve him of the troubling crate in his basement, and the Iranian would leave fifty million dollars in its place.

CHAPTER 34

Khalid Barghouti was a careful man. He had to be because he frequently travelled alone. But, when he checked into the Hotel Reina Sevillana he did not notice the middle-aged couple reading newspapers in a corner of the spacious lobby, and if he had, their gray hair and innocuous appearance would have signaled no cause for alarm.

He was thinking about the incredible power he was on the verge of acquiring. It would spread death and panic among the despised Jews and make the PJA the leading force for the eradication of Israel. The illegal occupation of his homeland would soon be ended.

Once the transfer had been made, the weapons would be loaded onto a motor launch on the Guadalquivir and transshipped to a Syrian ship waiting off the coast. He detested the idea of kowtowing to the Iranian money man, but the Shiites had proven helpful to his cause. Their mutual hatred of Israel united Sunni and Shiite.

But right now, Barghouti was tired. The indirect route he'd followed to get to Spain and the three-hour train ride from Madrid left him anxious to get to his room, take a shower, and lie down.

Had he not been distracted by his own thoughts,

he might have paid more attention when the gray-haired woman from the lobby followed him and the bellhop into the elevator and got off at the same floor.

The woman waited for them to turn into a corridor, then carefully followed at a distance, watching as Barghouti entered his room. She smiled at the retreating bellhop, waited until he was out of sight, and continued until she could note the number of Barghouti's room.

Ten minutes later, Michael listened to the voice of the female surveillant over the cell phone. Her real name was Levana Feldman. She had been born in Birmingham, England in 1950, and her parents immigrated to Israel in 1955. She'd been with the Mossad since 1978 and was one of the Office's most proficient surveillants along with her husband, Daniel.

"He's here," she said. "Room 375. He's cut his hair and shaved his beard, but it's Barghouti. No doubt about it."

"Do you think there's an empty room in the same corridor?" he asked.

"There should be. The hotel is not crowded. It's still a bit early in the season."

"Keep an eye on Barghouti if he goes out."

"Should I call in the "Irish" boys for reinforcements?"

"No, I'll call the girl and send her over to check into the hotel. We don't want the boys near there until showtime."

He closed the connection and leaned back in the chair and closed his eyes. It had begun, and now it must move forward without pause until completed. But the chances for success depended as much on the targets as the team.

Waiting.... Operations take time to unfold, and a lot of waiting is inevitable. Much of the time is devoted to thinking about how best to complete the mission, and for some operations even prayer comes into play. Michael Mossberg did his best to rectify what he was about to do with his sense of morality.

Spies engage in all sorts of activities, most of them dangerous, but *Kidon* operations often involve assassination, an activity that must be planned meticulously and conducted with ruthless precision. The Russians are past masters at targeted political assassination and are roundly condemned for it. Were *Kidon* assassinations any different from those carried out by the KGB?

Michael and his team intended to snuff out a human life, perhaps three human lives. They would do so with cold, impersonal meticulousness. Everything was planned so as to give their prey no chance of escape or defense. No one wanted a fair fight. They had never seen their targets before and had no personal animus against them. But they were targets, and they were to be eliminated. How could this be justified in a civilized world?

But Michael knew that all the eons of mankind's struggle had not yet produced universal enlightenment. His experience taught him to see the world as a jungle inhabited by feral beasts, many of which wish to devour Israel and erase the Jewish people from history. Barghouti and his confederates were such beasts, and Israel's survival required their eradication. In this case, Barghouti's life had to be weighed against the lives of hundreds, maybe thousands of Israelis.

Michael was nagged by a premonition of misfortune. Seville was a bad luck city for Jews, after all. It is a city of sparkling historical importance. But it also was the venue for the first *auto da fe* of the Spanish Inquisition and the beginning of the persecution of Jews in Spain. In 1492 Jews were expelled from the country to join the diaspora in exile.

There were too many moving parts, too many uncontrollable variables. The number of targets was a problem. To get them all, they would have to be taken together. Michael saw no way this could be done without considerable violence that would expose the team. David Shalev might be the interpreter of God's will, but in this instance the *memuneh* might be taking liberties with the Deity's wishes. To be completely successful, this mission would require Divine intervention.

A troubling variable was the chemical weapons themselves. The *memuneh* wanted to capture whatever the Russian was selling to Barghouti. But its location and description were unknown. The most likely place was the Russian's house, which was well-guarded.

The *Kidon* rule was to get in, complete the assignment, and get out undetected before any dead bodies they left behind were discovered. But to get to Gromov and the CBW weapons cache, they would have to go through his bodyguards which certainly would mean a firefight that would make a clean escape next to impossible.

One advantage of *Kidon* was that the Office ceded operational decisions in the field to the team leader. Michael opted to concentrate on one objective at a time. Eliminating Khalid Barghouti would simultaneously deprive the PJA of leadership and forestall the sale of chemical weapons to Israel's enemies. Maybe that would be enough for now. Barghouti was the prime target.

CHAPTER 35

The austere, dark man in the window seat stared vacantly at the sparse vegetation and sandy tan landscape of southern Spain as it rushed past. The AVE high speed train traveling at 300 kilometers per hour would take him in air-conditioned comfort from Madrid to Seville in three hours.

Adel Hatimi, with the rank of General, was second in command of VEVAK, *Vezarat-e Ettela'at va Amniat-e Keshvar*, the intelligence service of the Islamic Republic of Iran. He was a man of medium height and trim physique, befitting his military status. The narrow face with its sharp beak of a nose, eyes slightly too close together, and dark stubble of beard reminded one of Iran's president, Mahmoud Ahmadinejad. He was traveling on an alias passport that identified him as a businessman from Tehran.

Normally an officer of such rank would not be tasked with delivering funds to one of the many terrorist organizations supported by Iran. But this transaction was too important to leave to a subordinate. One of the mullahs' primary objectives was the destruction of Israel, and here was a way to strike at the very heart of the hated Jewish state.

The murder of Mehdi Asadi a few years earlier

had incensed him. More recently a researcher assigned to Project Amad, Iran's nuclear weapons development program, had met death in the same violent way. Hatimi and VEVAK were convinced that the Israelis were behind it all. This mission would avenge those insults without revealing Tehran's hand.

Interestingly, his Russian contacts had cautioned him against Sergei Gromov. Thus, he would proceed carefully and would not hand over the money without proof the chemical weapons actually existed. He would have to tamp down the Palestinian's enthusiasm, but the dog would obey the master.

He was anxious to conclude this business and return home. He was never comfortable outside Iran, and he missed his children. Most of his experience with foreigners was with the Russians. Unbelievers they may be, but their assistance to his country's nuclear and CBW programs, cooperation that had been initiated by the deceased Mehdi Asadi was irreplaceable.

The Palestinians were another matter entirely. They were a clever people, but easily led and avaricious. Hatimi was convinced the Palestinians would do anything for money, and it was with money that VEVAK controlled them. Hamas was under Tehran's thumb, and Arafat's cupidity knew no bounds. The filthy little sodomite diverted much PLO funding to secret foreign accounts.

Hatimi emerged from Seville's Santa Justa Station into the glaring day. He found the taxi queue and handed the driver a piece of paper with the name and address of the hotel. The heat of the Andalusian sun did not bother him, and the magnificent architecture of Seville did not impress him as they passed through the streets. All he wanted was to get to the hotel, conclude his business, and return home. He had a contact phone number to inform the Russian of his arrival.

With luck he would be on his way back to Tehran within a few days.

The wig and false moustache itched and made Michael feel self-conscious and slightly ridiculous, like a child made up for a school play. Any time he wore a disguise, he worried irrationally that it might fall off.

To the casual observer, the man checking into the Hotel Reina Sevillana was middle-aged, with a sprinkle of gray at his temples and a full moustache. He wore glasses with black, plastic frames. His suit was stylishly cut in the latest Madrid fashion, and his fluent Spanish left no doubt as to his nationality.

Señor Alfredo Morales had called earlier in the day and requested Room 374, which he said he had found pleasant during his last stay at the hotel. He had one heavy suitcase that the bellhop put on a trolley before leading him to the room. The bellhop was pleased with the 500-peseta tip, which was high for Spanish guests.

Michael Mossberg locked the door after the bellhop left and hefted the suitcase onto the bed. Inside, under a layer of clothing, were three Makarov pistols, their serial numbers eradicated, silencers, a black canvas bag, and a plastic case containing a syringe and an ampoule filled with liquid. Additionally, there was a variety of electronic gear and a laptop computer.

He then notified the "Irish" boys to come to his room. Barghouti was downstairs in the hotel dining room having lunch under the watchful eyes of the surveillance team. With luck, there could be enough time to gain access to the Palestinian's room. The team technician was already checked-in to the hotel and joined Michael. He began checking the equipment.

With the "Irish" boys standing watch in the corridor, the technician slipped a thin metal device attached by a thin wire to a black box into the key card slot in Barghouti's door. Lights flashed on the box, and within five minutes he had copied the code to open the door and transferred it to a blank card.

Inside Barghouti's room, a quick search revealed nothing more than the Palestinian's dirty laundry. Michael had not expected much more. The tech placed a listening device disguised as a block of wood under a table and a micro camera in one corner against the ceiling.

It would be a simple matter to wait for the Palestinian to return and surprise him then and there. It would be over in a matter of minutes, and the team would disperse.

Michael imagined returning home to Seriyah and their son and resuming a normal life. He wanted no more of *Kidon*, no more efficient, methodical killing, no more nerves on edge. But what was a "normal life" for an Israeli? With their backs to the Mediterranean and existential threats closing in on all sides, what choice did he have?

If the threat were to be annulled, the CBW weapons somehow must be neutralized. Gromov might find another buyer in Gaza or the West Bank. Michael had not yet come up with a plan to retrieve the CBW.

Just as they finished putting the room back as they had found it, Michael's cell phone vibrated. It was one of the surveillants downstairs. "Michael, two guys just met Barghouti in the lobby. They must be the Russian and the Iranian. They're on the way upstairs now. And there are three very tough looking guys with them, all of them armed if I don't miss my guess."

"Stand by downstairs in case they leave," ordered Michael.

He, the "Irish" boys, and the tech returned to Michael's room and gathered around the laptop as its screen lit up with a view of the interior of Barghouti's room.

There was the sound of movement in the corridor. On the screen four men entered the room. Michael squinted through the peep hole in his door and saw two burly men take up positions outside the Palestinian's door.

In response to a questioning look from the "Irish" boys, who were screwing silencers into the barrels of the Makarovs, Michael shook his head. "We could take them, but not without shots being fired and attracting attention. When we move, the action must be out of sight inside the room. For now, we'll wait to see what develops."

CHAPTER 36

Four men appeared on the computer screen. Barghouti was dressed casually in slacks and a white shirt open at the neck. This was the first time Michael had seen the Russian, a man in his mid-forties with thinning blond hair and the beginning of a paunch. He had a sharp face and gestured with his hands as he spoke. The Iranian was dark and thin and obviously uncomfortable. Michael had no idea who he was, but the sight of him brought back memories of the harrowing escape from Iran. The men remained standing as they talked, and their voices sounded tinny but clear over the short distance link.

Evidently, they had decided on English as their common language. Gromov spoke first. "Finally, we are all together, and I'm sure everyone wants to finish this business as quickly as possible." He looked expectantly at the Iranian, who did not identify himself.

"You are correct, Mr. Gromov," said the Iranian, "but there are conditions, the first of which is to verify the merchandise. I must examine it physically before the transaction can be completed. If I am satisfied, I will authorize the bank transfer, and Mr. Barghouti can take possession."

"Everything is prepared," said Barghouti with an

obsequious smile. "A ship is standing by off the coast and will send a boat to pick up the merchandise. I agree, we should conclude this matter as soon as possible." He turned his attention to Gromov. "I assume you have no objection to our friend's conditions?"

Gromov shook his head. "Of course not. It's a natural precaution. I assure you the merchandise is genuine, and I will be very happy when it is out of my house."

"Then you have no objection if we go there right now?" asked the Iranian.

"My car is outside," replied Gromov.

Michael's voice was soft. "Shit." As long as the group stayed together, with Gromov's three armed guards, there was no chance of a clean mission. No matter how many times he turned it over in his mind, a shoot-out on the streets of Seville was not in the cards, regardless of the stakes.

Gromov moved to the door, and the others followed, but the Iranian held up his hand. "Mr. Barghouti, there is no need for you to go with us now. While we are gone, you should notify the ship to be ready to launch the boat." He turned to the Russian. "As soon as I have verified the shipment and it has been delivered into the hands of Mr. Barghouti's colleagues, I will transfer the funds to your account."

Gromov studied him for a moment through slitted eyes. "You will, of course, remain with me until the transfer is made." His voice was calm, but the threat was implicit.

The Iranian did not like the idea, but there was no choice. He shrugged his shoulders and said, "Of course."

Barghouti started to protest, but the Iranian, already annoyed by the thought of being Gromov's temporary hostage, held up his hand again. "That is the way it will be." He shot a glance at the Russian. "If our friend here should fail to do as he says you will see to it that my people learn of it, and he will become a target of both of our organizations."

Barghouti stopped in his tracks and nodded. He stood and watched as Gromov led the Iranian out of the room followed by the bodyguard. Several minutes later the surveillance team informed Michael that the group had left the hotel.

Michael made a decision. "We move now," he said. "We can't let Barghouti make that call."

The Palestinian disappeared from the computer screen. Michael suspected the he had gone into the bathroom. He called one of the surveillants up from the lobby to stand guard in the corridor, then grabbed the medical kit and canvas bag and moved to the door, followed closely by the two "Irish" boys.

They used the duplicate key card to unlock Barghouti's door, moving as silently as possible. They had practiced this maneuver many times. Michael went in first, Makarov in hand, to find the room empty. The sound of a toilet flushing confirmed Barghouti's location. They moved quickly to the bathroom door where the "Irish" boys grabbed the Palestinian when he emerged. They clapped a hand over his mouth and held him as Michael inserted the needle of the syringe into a soft spot under his arm and pressed the plunger.

Barghouti would have felt a sting as the suxamethonium chloride was injected. He went limp within seconds as the paralysis brought on by the drug took effect. His panicked eyes remained open wide. The drug was a paralytic and did not induce unconsciousness.

As the "Irish" boys held him up Michael grabbed the helpless Palestinian's by the hair and jerked his head around so they were face to face. "Khalid Barghouti," he pronounced. "You have been judged and found guilty by the Israeli people of crimes against humanity. The sentence is death."

They laid the Palestinian, now completely immobilized, on the bed. Michael removed a portable defibrillator from the black canvas bag. The device had been specially modified by Mossad to override normal safety precautions and deliver a 200-joule shock that would induce a fatal fibrillation to a healthy heart. After three applications, Barghouti was dead. The suxamethonium chloride would be extremely difficult to detect. With luck, the death would be attributed to natural causes.

They then arranged the body on the bed and removed the electronic devices that had been planted earlier. Upon receiving the all clear from the surveillant, they returned to Michael's room.

It was still mid-afternoon, leaving several hours before the body might be discovered. The "Irish" boys left the hotel first, followed by the technician, and the remaining surveillants. Michael let a half-hour pass before he checked out.

Had he thought the Iranian might return, Michael would have kept the team in place. But the arrangement with Gromov nullified that. The operation was still incomplete, but he believed the most important target had been eliminated. Now, he would wait and further developments to dictate his actions.

He'd assigned the Frenchman, Marc LeBrun to follow the Russian and the Iranian when they left the hotel. Now his phone vibrated, and he saw LeBrun's call sign.

CHAPTER 37

Marc LeBrun followed the Russian's black Audi sedan and a follow-car carrying two bodyguards. As he pulled into traffic behind them, another dark sedan swerved in front and sped ahead. He ascribed this to normal Spanish driving habits until he noticed something strange. The sedan appeared to be following the Russian's cars too.

He kept a safe distance, hiding in traffic, and pulled into a vacant space with a view of the house. He watched as Gromov, the Iranian, and the three bodyguards entered the house, leaving the cars on the street. The sedan continued past the house and turned the corner. Maybe he'd been mistaken about someone else watching the Russian.

But a short time later, things started to happen. He called Michael.

"Michael," LeBrun's voice was excited over the phone. "Something weird is happening."

Directly across the street from the house was a flat, open space planted at regular intervals with young trees. Beyond this was the Guadalquivir River. Now, from the direction of the river a group of about a dozen men advanced rapidly. To LeBrun they looked like a SWAT team in dark uniforms and ballistic vests. All were armed.

He stared, fascinated, as they advanced on Gromov's house. Sentries were placed in the street to block access. LeBrun ducked behind the steering wheel but still had a good view. One sentry took up a position in the middle of the street about thirty feet away and brandished his weapon.

That's when LeBrun noticed something strange.

"What do you mean by 'weird?'" asked Michael.

"You're not going to believe it, but Gromov's house is under armed assault by a squad of guys in tactical gear."

As LeBrun watched, the main body of the group attacked the front door and stormed into the house. Within seconds a volley of gunshots rang out. It sounded like a full-fledged battle was raging inside the house.

"So, the Spanish are taking out Gromov?"

"That's what I thought at first," said LeBrun, "but now I'm not so sure. There's a road guard positioned near me, and he's carrying a *Vikhr* submachinegun."

"Are you sure?"

"Absolutely. You know who carries that weapon, and it sure as hell isn't the Spanish."

"Alpha Group." This was the FSB's special operations and counter-terrorism group. They were well-trained and ruthless. "Is it safe for you to stay and observe."

"I'm not moving. I don't think anyone has spotted me in the car. I'm about a half-block from the house."

"Good. Don't take any chances. You should get away before any Spanish cops arrive. We can't afford them holding you as a witness."

"It sounds like a shooting gallery," said LeBrun. "These guys aren't taking any prisoners."

"They must be after the CBW," guessed Michael. "It was stolen from a Russian arsenal."

"Yeah," said LeBrun. "Good for them, but there'll be a full-fledged battle if the Spanish cops show up."

Within ten minutes, the gunfire stopped. After what seemed like a long time but was actually five minutes LeBrun watched the assault team come out of the house. Two of their number appeared to be wounded or dead, carried by others with arms and legs dangling lifelessly. Two more came out carrying a large, wooden crate. The last two out the door dragged a disheveled man LeBrun recognized as the Iranian. The entire group rushed back across the open area and disappeared down the bank to the river. LeBrun rolled down the car window in time to hear the thrum of powerful engines.

People were poking their heads cautiously out of neighboring houses, and sirens sounded somewhere in the distance. LeBrun pulled into the street, did a U-turn, and cleared the area as fast as he could go.

CHAPTER 38

Adel Hatimi was not a happy man. Beside him in the rear seat of the large sedan, Gromov was silent, staring straight ahead. The Iranian was unaccustomed to being under the control of others, and he had developed an intense dislike for this man. His dealings with Russians thus far had been with officials, members of the SVR and FSB. Gromov, he knew, was a criminal, and he recalled the warnings he had received from Moscow.

Always a cautious man, Hatimi had requested traces on Gromov from the SVR *Rezident* in Tehran, explaining that he would soon be meeting him in Spain. The response had been immediate and surprisingly brusque: stay away from Gromov.

He ignored the warning because the opportunity to harm Israel was simply too promising. Nevertheless, his current position made him uncharacteristically nervous.

The cars drew to a stop in front of Gromov's house, and he was escorted inside. The place was voluptuously furnished. The Russian walked beside him. "I've let all the staff off for the day," he said, "to keep our business secret. To tell you the truth, I'll be only too happy when that stuff is out of my basement.

I'd almost pay you to take it off my hands." He laughed heartily at his own joke.

A door off the main corridor led to stairs down to the basement. Gromov switched on the lights. The large space boasted a wet bar and racks of wine against one wall. But the center of attention was a large wooden crate in the center of the floor. The crate carried Cyrillic markings. The lid had been removed and leaned against one side of the box.

Following Gromov, Hatimi looked inside and saw a metal container that looked like an ice chest with a hinged lid, also bearing Cyrillic markings he could not read.

"Go ahead," said Gromov, showing his teeth in a wicked smile. "Open it. Inspect the contents."

Hatimi hesitated for a second, then opened the metal lid. Inside, each nestled like a viper in a separate compartment were a dozen large aerosol canisters painted olive drab. The Iranian gingerly lifted one from its niche. It was not heavy. The top was fitted with what looked like a safety device, and there were no markings whatsoever. Everything matched what Hatimi had been told to expect by his own CBW experts.

He replaced the canister and turned to Gromov. "Very well, Mr. Gromov. I believe the merchandise is genuine. We should tell Mr. Barghouti and arrange for transfer to his boat tonight."

Gromov opened his mouth to speak but was interrupted by loud crash from upstairs, followed by the unmistakable sound of gunfire.

The Russian glared at Hatimi. "Are you double-crossing me? Do you think you can get away without paying me?"

Hatimi backed away from the enraged Russian who had drawn a very large pistol from his belt.

"I don't know what you're talking about," said Hatimi rapidly.

The gunfire drew closer as the two bodyguards upstairs fired their pistols. But this was met with a volley of automatic weapons fire. For a moment there was silence except for the tread of heavy boots on the floor upstairs. Then the basement door was shattered by a volley of bullets, and dark-clad men began pouring down the stairs.

As Hatimi retreated behind one of the wine racks, both Gromov and his bodyguard returned fire, striking one of the attackers on the stairs, but they were immediately cut down by multiple bullets. The attackers quickly filled the room. Hatimi recognized the language they were speaking as Russian which rendered him even more confused. He raised his hands, expecting at any moment to be the next to die.

A man who seemed to be in charge walked over and scrutinized him closely, comparing what he saw with a photograph he pulled from a pocket. In English he said, "You are General Adel Hatimi. You will come with us."

Before he could protest, two men grabbed Hatimi under the arms and dragged him toward the stairs.

On the floor a badly bleeding Gromov groaned and rolled onto his side. At a sign from the leader, one of the men stood over him and fired a bullet into his brain. He did the same with the bodyguard who probably was dead already.

"*Poshli,*" ordered the man in charge. "Let's get out of here."

Hatimi was almost in a trance. Everything happened so quickly, he could hardly believe it. Struggle as he might, he was no match for the men holding him. They dragged him upstairs, across the prostrate bodies of the other two bodyguards, and out of the house into the bright afternoon sunlight.

The group moved as one across the street toward the river and down the bank where two fast cigarette boats waited, their powerful twin motors revving. Handling the crate with great care, the men placed it in a boat. Hatimi was literally tossed in after it.

As soon as all were aboard, the boats sped to the center of the river and raced south toward the coast. Leaving white wakes at nearly sixty miles-per-hour they flew down the winding river passing cultivated fields on both banks, finally exiting into the Mediterranean and leaving the Chipiona lighthouse far behind.

Far out to sea they rendezvoused with a Russian fishing trawler. Its crane lifted the boats into its enormous hold. As the trawler got underway, the man who led the group approached Hatimi who sat on a bench near the rail.

"General, I apologize for the inconvenience, but be assured you are in no danger. Unfortunately, you ignored our warning to stay away from Gromov. We were under orders that no harm should come to you, but still, you were lucky. This ship will dock at our military base at Tartus where you will be met by Hezbollah representatives who will see to your return to Tehran. VEVAK has been informed. Moscow greatly regrets that you were in any way involved, but we could not permit these stolen weapons ever to be used. There are chemical signatures that inevitably would identify their origin."

Hatimi nodded glumly. Of course, the chemicals would be identified as Russian. The important thing had been to keep Iran's fingerprints off the operation. The Israelis could do nothing against Russia, but they could seek vengeance on Iran.

CHAPTER 39

As soon as he received Marc LeBrun's report, Michael ordered his team to disperse from Seville to a wide variety of planned destinations where they would be "dry cleaned" (exchange identity documents) before each returned to their normal locations. A week later, he was back in Tel Aviv, again sitting across the desk from David Shalev.

The events in Seville became an international sensation and the subject of broad speculation. So far, the death by an apparent heart attack of Khalid Barghouti had not been connected with the violence at Gromov's residence. In certain circles the Israelis were suspected of killing the Palestinian, but these circles always blamed the Israelis for everything. The Russian foreign ministry denied everything and suggested that the Spanish police were to blame. On the upside, the PJA was falling apart, some leaving of their own accord and others arrested by Israeli authorities.

Those who knew the truth in Moscow, Tehran, and Tel Aviv, and a few in Gaza were not talking. There was a lot of shame and blame to go around.

"Congratulations on completing a difficult task," said Shalev.

Michael nodded. "Do we know what happened to

the Iranian?"

"Ah, the Iranian. He was General Adel Hatimi of VEVAK. Our sources tell us he was turned over to Hezbollah in Syria and is now back in Tehran, no doubt somewhat the wiser about collaborating with the Russians." Shalev chuckled. "They can always be counted on to prefer blunt force to finesse. They were lucky to get away with that show in Seville. I'm trying to think of a way to tie them to it."

"They'll never admit they lost CBW materials, let alone that they even have them."

"Oh, I think everyone knows they still have them, given all the revelations after the Soviet Union fell. At least it seems that Yeltsin is trying to do some things right. I hope he succeeds."

"That's probably a forlorn hope, *memuneh*."

"Sad, but true." Shalev looked more tired than ever, and Michael was ashamed of any thought of abandoning the Mossad. Men like Shalev carried the weight of Israeli survival on their shoulders, and he marveled at Shalev's resilience. How could he do less?

Plus ça change

Evil, it seemed, always would be with them.

CHAPTER 40

Tel Aviv - 2018

The sunlight streaming through the window caught the layers of blue smoke drifting throughout the room like storm clouds gathering in the sky. This was appropriate to the *memuneh's* gloomy mood.

Eitan Ronan leaned back in the desk chair, making it creak, and blew more smoke into the air. He still favored Gauloise, and to hell with anyone who complained about it. He was the *memuneh* now, and he would do as he pleased for as long as God saw fit to permit it. His thick hair was now gray rather than black, his body was not as hard as it once had been, and some pounds had been added. But his fierceness had not diminished.

The office was his now and had been for several years. David Shalev, Ronan's wise and ruthless mentor, had long ago gone to his Maker, and sometimes he envied him. Like his predecessor, Ronan fervently hoped there was no such place as hell.

But if the flames of perdition existed, he was certain there were others who would be far ahead of him in line to enter the fiery gates. There was a slight chance he would make the cut to go in the other direction.

A few weeks earlier the Syrians had used chemical weapons, probably chlorine and sarin this time, against helpless civilians on the outskirts of Damascus. It was by far not the first time and likely not the last time they would do so. The Western democracies had long lacked the courage necessary to put down the Assad regime and its Russian and Iranian backers. But now, at least, the new American Administration, the Brits and French had shown their teeth by raining cruise missiles onto Syrian targets.

Of course, the Syrians had long had a well-developed CBW capability, and the missiles required to deliver it. The missiles had been based in Aleppo, Soviet supplied missiles to be sure – SCUDs, and FROGs, and SCARABs. But it was not only the Soviets who enabled them; plenty of help was forthcoming from western suppliers happy to provide the necessary materials, and even set up chemical factories. Money talked, and western governments chose to look the other way. After all, it was mainly a problem for the Jews. The only thing that had prevented Assad's father from employing these weapons against Israel was the certain knowledge that there would be instant retaliation, maybe in the form of nuclear strikes.

It had been the same with Saddam Hussein whose CBW stores had been either transported to Syria or confiscated by terrorists after he was gone. Both Iraq and Iran had resorted to such weapons during their long, torturous war, and Saddam had used it mercilessly against the Kurds at Halabja in 1988, killing 5,000 people.

Now engaged in a bloody civil war, Assad was

content to murder his own people with no regard for public opinion. He had the Russians and the Iranians to back him up, and the Western Allies had thus far proven powerless to stop them.

The Russians did not seem to care that they had become international pariahs, brazenly murdering people in the heart of the United Kingdom with polonium and only a few weeks earlier with a nerve agent developed long ago in Soviet labs – novichok.

They had been overly optimistic, Ronan and Shalev, nearly three decades earlier when they had worried about Russia exporting CBW to Iran. In truth, they had accomplished little. The Iranian CBW program was strong. In sophisticated underground facilities in the northern city of Sahid Bahonar, 38 Iranian and 12 Russian scientists worked to develop CBW warheads for Iran's missiles. Ronan worried that the Iranians were crazy enough not to be concerned about nuclear annihilation. Even closer to home, the Iranians were establishing military bases in Syria, a problem the IDF might have to resolve in violent fashion that would risk a dangerous confrontation with the mullahs' regime.

Michael Mossberg's assignment in Iran had not been entirely in vain. Following David Shalev's strategy of at least slowing down Iran's development of weapons of mass destruction, the Mossad had infiltrated teams that had carried out numerous assassinations of Iranian nuclear scientists and technicians. And, of course, the IDF had targeting data for all Iranian strategic facilities, including Sahid Bahonar.

Evil, it seemed, always would be with them. The same actors were addicted to it: Russia, China, Iran, Syria, North Korea, and several minor players. If these countries did not have real external enemies, the ruling regimes had to invent them to keep their populations in line, and Israel was a popular scapegoat. And just as a lioness guards her cubs, Israel must defend herself.

They lived in a dangerous neighborhood with the Axis of Evil running right through it. The future was uncertain. Ronan lit another Gauloise and turned back to the papers on his desk and to the task of buying his country another day of life.

THE END

References:

1. **John Ellis, "This Is What Scares US Military Strategists Most," <u>Business Insider</u>, February 2, 2011.**

The latest batch of Wikileaks cables <u>is out.</u> They show acute concerns about the possibility of a rogue state nuclear attack, the possibility of Al Qaeda building radioactive dirty bombs and the possibility of Al Qaeda acquiring a nuclear weapon. As well, they fret about rogue states and terrorist groups getting their hands on biological and chemical weaponry (CBW).

CBW is what keeps US military strategists up at night. During the George H.W. Bush administration, it was learned that the Soviet Union had embarked on a vast biological weapons program. At its peak, the program employed over 22,000 people, virtually all of them focused on weaponizing genetically-modified biological agents. This work was described in terrifying detail in Richard Preston's classic work, "<u>Demon in the Freezer.</u>" The program produced a lot of "intellectual capital" for building biological weapons.

After the Soviet Union collapsed, the people who held that "intellectual capital" (in their brains) dispersed, only to re-emerge a few years later in places like Syria, North Korea, Iraq and Iran. U.S. intelligence spent vast sums tracking these bio-weaponeers. Many were offered jobs in the

U.S. But too many remained "at large."

The effort to track down former Soviet bio-weaponeers went into overdrive after 9/11. A global manhunt was undertaken. Countries around the globe contributed to the effort.

The effort was quite successful. But disturbing reports continued to fill the President's Threat Matrix report, the daily intelligence briefing on how the world might end.

Later on in the George W. Bush administration, a package was delivered to the President's science advisor. It detailed how, using strings of molecules purchased from the back pages of science magazines, one could create a genetically modified polio virus. Vaccination would be no defense. This virus would EZ-pass right through it.

As it happens, the men who put together the genetically-modified polio virus were prominent scientists, well known in the world of biology and genomics. They posed no threat. But what if the package had scientifically described a genetically-modified weaponized smallpox, which could be contracted by twelve suicide spreaders, their only task to cough on people in public places?

What could the military do about that? Smallpox takes some time to incubate. The suicide spreaders could wander around O'Hare for two days, looking perfectly healthy, and no one would be the wiser. A day or two after that, they would begin to get very, very sick. By the seventh day, they would probably be dead.

But in the early days, by coughing a lot, they would be spreading the virus at a central node of American transportation. No "ring" strategy (surround the virus and cut off its spread) would be possible.

This is the U.S. military's "nightmare scenario." If North Korea tries to launch a nuclear attack, it will be destroyed in 24 hours. If Al Qaeda puts a dirty bomb in the Paris Metro, it'll be open season on them. The order will be: shoot first, ask questions later and don't sweat collateral damage.

But if someone puts genetically-modified weaponized smallpox into general circulation, it won't even be clear who did it, at least initially. And there is literally no defense. People have to breath.

This is asymmetrical warfare at its most acute. You don't need to read Wikileaks to know that it's pretty much all anyone in the military thinks about when they think about future threats.

2. **Nitsana Darshan-Leitner and Samuel M. Katz, "HARPOON – Inside the Covert War Against Terrorism's Money Masters," ISBN 978-0-316-39902-9, Hachette Books, November 2017.**

A revelatory account of the cloak-and-dagger Israeli campaign to target the finances fueling terror organizations--an effort that became the blueprint for U.S. efforts to combat threats like ISIS and drug cartels.

ISIS boasted $2.4 billion of revenue in 2015, yet

for too long the global war on terror overlooked financial warfare as an offensive strategy. "Harpoon," the creation of Mossad legend Meir Dagan, directed spies, soldiers, and attorneys to disrupt and destroy money pipelines and financial institutions that paid for the bloodshed perpetrated by Hamas, Hezbollah, and other groups. Written by an attorney who worked with Harpoon and a bestselling journalist, Harpoon offers a gripping story of the Israeli-led effort, now joined by the Americans, to choke off the terrorists' oxygen supply, money, via unconventional warfare.

(From https://www.amazon.com/Harpoon-Inside-Against-Terrorisms-Masters-ebook/dp/B06XR93Q1T/ref=sr_1_1?s=books&ie=UTF8&qid=1524068007&sr=1-1&keywords=HARPOON)

3. **Jonathan B. Tucker, "Bioweapons from Russia: Stemming the Flow," Issues in Science and Technology, Volume XV Issue 3, Spring 1999.**

"For nearly two decades, the former Soviet Union and then Russia maintained an offensive biological warfare (BW) program in violation of an international treaty, the 1972 Biological and Toxin Weapons Convention. In addition to five military microbiological facilities under the control of the Soviet Ministry of Defense (MOD), a complex of nearly 50 scientific institutes and production facilities worked on biological weapons under the cover of the Soviet Academy of Sciences, the Ministry of Agriculture, the

Ministry of Health, and an ostensibly civilian pharmaceutical complex known as Biopreparat. The full magnitude of this top-secret program was not revealed until the defection to the West of senior bioweapons scientists in 1989 and 1992."

See full article at:

http://www.jstor.org/stable/43313926?seq=1#page_scan_tab_contents)

4. **"Issues in Science and Technology," Volume XV Issue 3, Spring 1999, "Bioweapons from Russia: Stemming the Flow," by Jonathan B. Tucker.**

"For nearly two decades, the former Soviet Union and then Russia maintained an offensive biological warfare (BW) program in violation of an international treaty, the 1972 Biological and Toxin Weapons Convention. In addition to five military microbiological facilities under the control of the Soviet Ministry of Defense (MOD), a complex of nearly 50 scientific institutes and production facilities worked on biological weapons under the cover of the Soviet Academy of Sciences, the Ministry of Agriculture, the Ministry of Health, and an ostensibly civilian pharmaceutical complex known as Biopreparat. The full magnitude of this top-secret program was not revealed until the defection to the West of senior bioweapons scientists in 1989 and 1992."

5. *Barton Gellman*

"In the field of biological weapons, there is almost no prospect of detecting a pathogen until it has been used in an attack."

6. **Reza Kahlili**

"A Time to Betray – The Astonishing Double Life of a CIA Agent inside the Revolutionary Guard of Iran" – Threshold Editions, 2010

ACKNOWLEDGEMENTS

First my unbounded gratitude goes out to those readers who have enjoyed my books, as I hope they will enjoy this one.

As always, thanks go to my family who do their best to remain patient as I suffer frequent bouts of writer's block, about which I grumble and complain. Sometimes, as was the case with this book, the condition affects me for months.

My many friends who share the burden and experience of writing fiction are wonderful sources of inspiration. I am especially indebted to Jake Needham, who has been unstintingly generous in his offers of advice and encouragement. Jake also steered me to a wonderful cover artist, Rena Hoberman.

Special thanks to my high-school classmate, Judy Williams, who bravely offered to proof-read the manuscript of "Buy Another Day" and who offered suggestions to make the story better.

A Russian exile who shall remain nameless was kind enough to provide background information from the Russian language media on the 1979 "Sverdlovsk Incident." There is a great deal of English language information on this incident, as well.

This book begins with a fictionalized account of the "Sverdlovsk Incident" of March - April 1979. There is an abundance of material in several languages describing the incident, and perhaps Russian press accounts from the early 1990's are the best. Just as with this section of "Buy Another Day," the other vignettes herein are based on actual incidents in which

Mossad *Kidon* activity is suspected or known. I have, of course, taken many liberties. All the characters are completely fictional, creations of the imagination, and readers of my past novels will recognize several old friends.

It is important to remember that the action in Iran takes place at the beginning of the 1990's. At that time, a semi-autonomous Kurdistan had been declared in northeastern Iraq and was under the protection of U.S. and allied forces. Much has changed since then.

The conditions inside Tehran's notorious Evin Prison are derived from descriptions in Reza Khalili's excellent book, "A Time to Betray," and I have every reason to believe the description is accurate. I highly recommend Khalili's book to anyone interested in learning the true nature of the regime in Iran.

The morality of political assassination is a sub-text of this story. It is up to the reader to decide how he or she feels about assassination. Even the thought of killing another human being is abhorrent to most of us except in time of war. It is all too easy to draw moral equivalency between the acts fictionally ascribed in this book to *Kidon* and, for example, the well-known Russian penchant for assassinating political enemies. Obviously, I am sympathetic to Israel's struggle against terrorism sponsored by entities that wish for nothing less than the annihilation of the State of Israel and her people. I believe that violent measures against such an existential enemy are fully justified.

Michael R. Davidson
New Market, VA, May 2018

All of Michael R. Davidson's books
may be found at:

michaelrdavidson.com

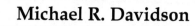

Made in the USA
Lexington, KY
26 March 2019